To:
Johnny McDonald

From: Marlene Eisenhart
Christmas 1972

GREAT GHOST STORIES
of the
OLD WEST

Edited by BETTY BAKER

FOUR WINDS PRESS · NEW YORK

CONTENTS

———◆———

The Western Writers of America is an organization of professional authors whose aims are to promote their common interests, encourage the writing of better-quality Westerns, and bring them more effectively to the attention of the reading public. The contributors to this volume are all members of the Western Writers of America.

GREAT GHOST STORIES
of the
OLD WEST

INTRODUCTION

———————•—•———————

Ghostly history is as old as man's. Ghosts gathered in the shadows of prehistoric caves, walked drafty halls in ancient castles, and creaked the stairs of colonial homes. Wherever man has journeyed, ghosts have followed.

They crossed the Bering Strait with the ancestors of the Indians. They whisked across the Atlantic with the Jamestown settlers. And when Americans packed their Conestoga wagons and headed West, ghosts moved with them.

But the land west of the Mississippi River was unlike any seen before by man or ghost. The lonely windswept prairies led on forever. Strange desert plants took human form in the moonlight, and mesas rose like forbidden islands in seas of tinted sand, endlessly changing with the movement of sun and cloud. Water-carved rocks took weird shapes. Gigantic mountains blocked the trails, with cliffs and wooded canyons that moaned in the wind. If ever a land was created for haunting, it was the American West.

It was also a harsh land, one that made its own rules. Men who could live happily by them were mavericks, individuals as strange and varied as the landscape itself. Small wonder that the ghosts were mavericks, too.

No clanking dungeon chains or wafting through dusty corridors for Western ghosts! Occasionally one took refuge in the bell tower of a ruined Spanish mission or the parade ground of a deserted Army fort. Few buildings, however, are haunted in the West. The Indians destroyed their homes rather than risk a haunting, but it probably wasn't necessary. Whole mining towns have been left to the spectres, but few spooks walk the so-called ghost towns. For as a general rule, Western ghosts, like the men they followed, preferred the rugged outdoors.

Ghosts gathered around the campfires of the mountain men, joining ancient Indian spirits and those brought by the Spanish conquistadors. Cowboy ghosts followed spectral trail herds, riding phantom stallions. Ghosts prowled abandoned mines and guarded forgotten treasure. There were even haunted railroads, though it's been years since anyone has reported a ghost upon the tracks. Passenger trains are too few and the diesel engines too swift.

Besides, ghosts don't care to mix with superhighways, neon lights, glass-sided skyscrapers, and jet planes. Ghosts need drafty houses, deep shadows, and country quiet enough for the wind to be heard. They can't compete with TV sets and transistor radios. The big creaky houses they loved are disappearing. And so are the ghosts.

But in the desert, the windswept mesas and canyons

of the West, a few phantoms still linger. A lonely campfire will draw them to hear their stories retold. The solitary camp is giving way to camping trailers, crowded national parks and motels. Highways invade the remotest sections of the West. And the ghosts retreat.

Before they disappear forever, the Western Writers of America have tracked down some of the most famous of the Western ghosts. In their stories, one can trace the history of the American West and the men who tamed it. They were adventurers, tough and impulsive, doggedly challenging the hardships of the rugged terrain they called home.

There were men like Canady in "The Trap," solitary mavericks who found in the plains and canyons of the American West a refuge from the world of men and the rules of society. It is not surprising that Canady's eerie, inexplicable story involves him in a mystical conspiracy with the strange and ruthless land he has chosen.

New Mexico and the Spanish heritage in which so much of Western history is rooted come to life in "Ghost Wolf of Thunder Mountain" and "Back Before the Moon." In different ways, these suspenseful tales reveal the exotic supernatural world that Spanish frontiersmen found in the mesas of the West.

"The Hexer" gives glimpses into the domestic life of the early settlers. It tells of the great influx of families who left their homes in the East to seek a better life in the unexplored territory west of the Mississippi River. First they answered the call of gold in California; later they discovered the rich soil of the valleys and swamps. These men were not the mavericks, the loners; they brought their families and began to carve a community and a civilization out of the wilderness. The ghostly events surrounding the hexer in this story have a totally different impact than those in the other tales.

Perhaps the most essential and often least explored character in the drama of the American West is the American Indian. "The Strange Valley" is a mind-twisting tale about three young Sioux Indians. In the middle of the narration, the story makes a shocking about-face, jolting the reader's sense of time and place. This arbitrary leap may correspond to the change experienced by the Indians of the West; suddenly strange white settlers began seizing their territory, transforming it to suit new and mysterious uses, and leaving them disinherited in their own country. Past ghosts and present realities become strangely confused in this mystifying story.

The two remaining legends have the robust spirit of the frontier adventurer. In "Johnny Who Rode The Ghost Train," young Johnny is a gold-seeker, that stubborn breed of American who flocked to California in the hopes of striking it rich. Cholla, in "The White Riders," is an old-time cowboy, most famous of the Western heroes. Their uncanny experiences derive from the classic and terrifying moment of being stranded, completely alone and without water, on the immense deserts of the West. The mysterious adventures that await these two men embody the romance and suspense of the frontier.

In this volume, American ghosts are once again brought to life, reminding the modern reader of the otherworldly magic that continues to pervade the American plains, a magic which is as old as the West itself.

Betty Baker

THE STRANGE VALLEY

By T. V. Olsen

The three horsemen came up on the brow of a hill, and the valley was below them. It was a broad cup filled by the brooding thickness of the prairie night. The light shed by a narrow sickle of moon picked out just another Dakota valley, about a mile across as the white men reckoned distance, and surrounded by a rim of treeless hills. The valley floor was covered by an ordinary growth of a few small oaks, a lot of brush, and some sandy flats with a sparse lacing of buffalo grass.

Young Elk said, "Is this what you wish us to see, Blue Goose?" He made no effort to keep the skepticism from his voice.

"Yes," said the rider on his left. "This is the place."

"Now that we're here, tell us again what you saw the other night." The third youth, the shaman's son, sounded very intent. "From where did it come?"

"From there." Blue Goose leaned forward as he pointed toward the eastern end of the valley. "As I told you, I'd had a long day of hunting, and I was very tired. I made my camp in the center of the valley, and fell asleep at once. This was about sunset.

"It was long after dark when I woke. I came awake all at once, and I don't know why. I heard a strange sound, a kind of growl that was very low and steady, and it was a long way off. But it was running very fast in my direction, and I sat in my blanket and waited."

Young Elk said with a grim smile, "Because you were too afraid even to run."

Blue Goose was silent for a moment. "Yes," he said honestly. "I was afraid. I didn't know what the thing was, but I knew it was getting closer. And growling louder all the while, as if in great pain or anger. Then I saw it.

"It was a huge beast, as big as a small hill, black in the night and running very close to the ground, and its two eyes were yellow and glaring. It went past me very close, but so fast I didn't think it saw me. It was bellowing as loud as a hundred bull buffaloes if they all bellowed at once. Suddenly it was gone."

"What do you mean, it was gone?" Young Elk demanded. "You said that before."

"I'm not sure. All I know is that suddenly I saw it no more and heard it no more."

"I wish you could tell us more about it," said the shaman's son. "But I suppose it was very dark."

"Yes," Blue Goose agreed. "Even a little darker than tonight." He hesitated. "I thought that the thing might be covered with scales—bright scales like a huge fish—since the moon seemed to glint on it here and there. But I couldn't be sure."

"You're not very sure of anything," Young Elk gibed.

Blue Goose sighed. "I do not know what I saw. As I have said, I left the valley very fast and camped a long way off that night. But I came back in the morning. I looked for the thing's spoor. I looked all over, and there was nothing. Yet I found where I had camped, and my pony's tracks and my own. But the thing left no sign at all."

"Because there had never been a thing. You should be more careful about what you eat, my friend." Young Elk spoke very soberly, though he felt like laughing out loud. "Spoiled meat in one's belly is like *mui waken*, the strong drink. It has a bad effect on the head."

For a little while the three young Sioux sat their ponies in silence, looking down into the dark stillness of the valley. A silky wind pressed up from the valley floor, a wind warm with the summer night and full of the ripening smells of late summer.

But something in it held a faint chill, and that was strange. Young Elk felt a crawl of gooseflesh on his bare shoulders, and he thought: *The night is turning cold, that is all.* He felt the nervous tremor run through his mount.

He laid his hand on the pony's shoulder and spoke quietly to the animal. He was angry at Blue Goose, his best friend, for telling this foolish story and angry at himself for coming along tonight with the other two because he was deeply curious. And back in their camp only a few miles to the north there was firelight and laughter and a warm-eyed girl named Morning Teal, and Young Elk was a fool to be out here with his friend and with the son of that tired old faker of a medicine man.

Of late, Young Elk thought sourly, there had been more than the usual quota of wild stories of visions and bad spirits running rampant among the people. Early this same summer, on the river of the Greasy Grass that the whites called Little Big Horn, the long-haired General Custer had gone down to defeat and death with his troops. Many warriors of their own band had been among the twelve thousand Sioux, Cheyenne, and Arapaho who had helped in the annihilation of a hated enemy.

In the uneasy weeks since, as the people followed the buffalo, hunting and drying meat in the prospect of being driven back to the reservation by white cavalry, a rash of weird happenings were reported. Men who had died were seen walking the prairie with bloody arrows protruding from them. Voices of the dead were heard in the night wind. It was the shaman's part to encourage this sort of nonsense. A man claimed that a bluecoat soldier he had scalped appeared to him nightly with the blood still fresh on his head. The shaman chanted gibberish and told him to bury the scalp so that the ghost would trouble his nights no more.

Young Elk was disgusted. He had never seen even one of these spirits. Only the fools who believed in such things ever saw them.

The shaman's son broke the long pause, speaking quietly. "This valley is a strange place. Today I spoke with my father and told him what Blue Goose has told us. He said that he knows of this place, and that his father's fathers knew of it too. Many strange things happened here in the old days. Men known to be long dead would be seen walking—not as spirits, but in the flesh. Still other things were seen, things too strange to be spoken of. Finally all our people of the *Lakotas* came to shun the valley. But that was so long ago that even most of the old ones have forgotten the stories."

Young Elk made a rude chuckling sound with his tongue and teeth.

"Young Elk does not believe in such things," the shaman's son observed. "Why then did he come with us tonight?"

"Because otherwise for the next moon I would hear nothing from you and Blue Goose but mad stories about what you saw tonight. I'd prefer to see it for myself."

"Oh," said Blue Goose, "then there *was* something? I did not make this great story out of the air?"

"Maybe not." Young Elk said slyly, "Maybe it was the white man's iron horse that Blue Goose saw."

"Now you jest with me. Even though I am not all-wise like Young Elk, still I know that the iron horse of the *wasicun* runs on two shining rails, and there are no rails here. And the iron horse does not growl thus, nor does it have two eyes that flame in the dark."

Another silence stretched among the three youths as they sat their ponies on the crest of the hill and peered down into the dark valley. And Young Elk thought angrily, *What is this?* They had come here to go down in the valley and wait in the night, in hopes that the thing Blue Goose had seen would make another appearance. Yet they all continued to sit here as though a winter of the spirit had descended and frozen them all to the spot.

Young Elk gave a rough laugh. "Come on!" He kneed his pony forward, down the long grassy dip of hill. The others followed.

Near the bottom, Young Elk's pony turned suddenly

skittish, and he had to fight the shying animal to bring him under control. Blue Goose and the shaman's son were having trouble with their mounts too.

"This is a bad omen," panted the shaman's son. "Maybe we had better go back."

"No," Young Elk said angrily, for his pony's behavior and the strange feeling of the place were putting an edge on his temper. "We've come this far, and now we'll see what there is to see, if anything. Where was Blue Goose when he thought he saw the beast?"

Blue Goose said, "We must go this way," and forced his horse through a heavy tangle of chokecherry brush. He led the way very quickly, as though afraid that his nerve would not hold much longer.

They came to a rather open stretch of sand flats that caught a pale glimmer of moonglow; it was studded with clumps of thicket and a few scrub oaks. "Here is the place," Blue Goose told them.

The three Sioux settled down to wait. Nobody suggested that it would be more comfortable to dismount. Somehow it seemed better to remain on their ponies and accept a cramp or two. It was only, Young Elk told himself, that they should be ready for anything, and they might have a sudden need of the ponies.

Once more it was the shaman's son who ended an interval of silence. "What time of the night did it happen, Blue Goose?"

"I can't be sure. But close to this time, I think."

Silence again. The ponies shuffled nervously. The wind hushed through some dead brush, which rattled like dry, hollow bird bones. Idly Young Elk slipped his throwing-ax from his belt and toyed with it. He slid his hand

over the familiar shape of the flint head and the fresh
thongs of green rawhide that lashed it to the new handle
he had put on only this morning. His palm felt moist.

And his head felt slightly dizzy. Now the shapes of
rocks, the black masses of brush, seemed to shimmer and
swim; the landscape seemed misty and unreal as if seen
through a veil of fog, yet there was no fog. *It is a trick of
the moon,* Young Elk thought. He gripped the ax tighter;
his knuckles began to ache.

"There!" Blue Goose whispered. "Do you hear it?"

Young Elk snapped, "I hear the wind," but even as
the words formed on his lips the sound was increasing,
unmistakably not the wind. Not even a gale wind roaring
through the treetops of a great forest made such a noise.
As yet he could see nothing, but he knew that the sound
was moving in their direction.

Suddenly the two yellow eyes of which Blue Goose
had spoken came boring out of the night. Now he could
see the hulking black shape of the monster running toward
them at an incredible speed and so low to the ground that
its legs could not be seen. All the while the strange humming roar it made was steadily growing.

The ponies were plunging and rearing with fear. The
shaman's son gave a cry of pure panic and achieved
enough control over his mount to kick it into a run. In a
moment Blue Goose bolted after him.

Young Elk fought his terrified pony down and held
the trembling animal steady, his own fear swallowed in an
eagerness to have a closer look at the thing. But he was
not prepared for the fury of its rush as it bore down toward him. And its round, glaring eyes blinded him—he
could see nothing beyond them.

It let out a piercing, horrible shriek as it neared him—it was hardly the length of three ponies away—and it seemed to hesitate. It hissed at him, a long gushing hiss, while the yellow eyes bathed him in their wicked glare.

Young Elk waited no longer. He lunged his pony in an angling run that carried him past the thing's blunt snout, and in that moment brought his arm back and flung the ax with all his strength. He heard it make a strange hollow boom, although he did not see it hit, and then he was racing on through the brush, straining low to his pony's withers, heedless of the tearing branches.

Young Elk did not slow down till he reached the end of the valley; then he looked back without stopping. There was no sign of the beast. The valley was deserted and quiet under the dim moonlight.

Young Elk crossed the rim of hills and caught up with his friends on the prairie beyond. "Did you see it?" the shaman's son demanded eagerly.

"No. Its eyes blinded me. But I hit it with my ax." Young Elk paused; his heart was pounding so fiercely in his chest he was afraid they would hear it, so he went quickly on, "I heard the ax hit the thing. So it was not a ghost."

"How do you know?" countered the shaman's son. "Where did it go? Did you see?"

"No," Young Elk said bitterly. "It was very fast."

"Let's go back to camp," Blue Goose said. "I don't care what the thing was. I do not want to think about it."

Joe Kercheval had been dozing in his seat when his partner, Johnny Antelope, hit the brakes of the big truck

22

and gave Joe a bad jolt. And then Joe nearly blew his stack when Johnny told him the reason he had slammed to an abrupt stop on this long, lonely highway in the middle of nowhere.

"I tell you, I saw him," Johnny insisted as he started up again and drove on. "A real old-time Sioux buck on a spotted pony. He was sitting on his nag right in the middle of the road, and I almost didn't stop in time. Then he came charging past the cab, and I saw him fling something—I think it was an ax—at the truck. I heard it hit. You were waking up just then—you must have heard it."

"I heard a rock thrown up by the wheels hit somewheres against the trailer, that's all," Joe said flatly. "You been on the road too long, kid. You ought to lay off a few weeks, spend a little time with your relatives on the reservation."

Johnny Antelope shook his head. "I saw him, Joe. And then I didn't see him. I mean—I could swear he disappeared—simply vanished into thin air—just as he rode past the cab. Of course it was pretty dark. . . ."

"Come off it. For a college-educated Indian, you get some pretty far-out notions. I've made this run a hundred times and I never seen any wild redskins with axes, spooks or for real."

"You white men don't know it all, Joe. You're Johnny-come-latelies. This has been our country for a long, long time, and I could tell you some things. . . ." Johnny paused, squinting through the windshield at the racing ribbon of highway unfolding in the tunneling brightness of the headlights. "I was just remembering. This is a stretch of land the Sioux have always shunned.

There are all kinds of legends concerning it. I remember one story in particular my old granddaddy used to tell us kids—I guess he told it a hundred times or more . . ."

"Nuts on your granddaddy."

Johnny Antelope smiled. "Maybe you're right, at that. Old Blue Goose always did have quite an imagination."

"So does his grandson." Joe Kercheval cracked his knuckles. "There's a turn-off just up ahead, kid. Swing around there."

"What for, Joe?"

"We're going back to where you seen that wild man on a horse. I'm gonna prove to you all you seen was moonshine." Joe paused, then added wryly, "Seems like I got to prove it to myself, too. I say it was just a rock that hit the truck, and I'll be losin' sleep if I don't find out for sure."

Without another word Johnny swung the big truck around and headed back east on the highway. The two truckers were silent until Johnny slowed and brought the truck to a shrieking stop. The air brakes were still hissing as he leaned from the window, pointing. "Here's the spot, Joe. I recognize that twisted oak on the right."

"Okay, let's have a close look." They climbed out of the cab, and Johnny pointed out the exact spot where he had first seen the Indian warrior, and where the warrior had cut off the highway alongside the cab and thrown his ax.

"Look here, kid." Joe played his flashlight beam over the roadside. "Soft shoulders. If your boy left the concrete right here, his horse would of tromped some mighty deep prints in the ground. Not a sign, see?"

"Wait a minute," Johnny Antelope said. "Flash that torch over here, Joe." He stooped and picked up something from the sandy shoulder.

The halo of light touched the thing Johnny held in his outstretched hand. "Know what this is, Joe?" he asked softly. "A Sioux throwing-ax."

Joe swallowed. He started to snort, "Nuts. So it's an ax . . ." but the words died on his lips.

For under the flashlight beam, even as the two men watched, the wooden handle of the ax was dissolving into rotted punk, and the leather fastenings were turning cracked and brittle, crumbling away. Only the stone blade remained in Johnny's hand, as old and flinty and weathered as if it had lain there by the road for an untold number of years. . . .

THE PHANTOM MUSTANG

By S. Omar Barker

Wherever pounding hoof-beats drum,
As galloping riders go or come,
Wherever the saddle is still a throne,
And the dust of hoofs by wind is blown,
Wherever are horsemen, young or old,
The pacing mustang's tale is told:

A hundred years, on hill and plain,
With comet tail and flying mane,
Milk-white, free, and high of head,
Over the range his trail has led.

27

Never a break in his pacing speed,
Never a trot nor a lope his need,
Since faraway days of the wagon train,
Men have followed his trail in vain.

A score of horses spurred to the death.
Still he flees like a phantom's breath,
And from some hill at horizon's hem,
Snorts his challenge back at them.

A bullet drops him dead by day,
Yet white at night he speeds away.
Forever a thief of tamer steeds,
Stallion prince of the mustang breeds,
Coveted prize of the men who ride—
Never a rope has touched his hide.

Wherever the saddle is still a throne,
The great white mustang's tale is known.

O Phantom Ghost of Heart's Desire,
Lusty limbed, with soul of fire,
Milk-white monarch, may you, free,
Race the stars eternally!

THE TRAP

By Clay Fisher

Canady felt the horse beginning to go rough beneath him. He had been expecting it. On this rocky going, no mount could make it for long when he was already ridden out in coming to it.

"Easy, easy," he said to the laboring animal. "It's only a posse." The horse seemed to understand the tone of the words, for it slowed and went better and steadier for a ways. "We'll rest on the rise ahead," Canady said. "I can see back a few miles and you can catch some wind and we'll go on. We'll make it."

He knew they wouldn't. He knew it before they came to the rise and he got down and walked out on the over-hanging spur of gray-black basalt that gave a view down the canyon behind them for ten miles. It wasn't a canyon, really, but a narrowing valley. The canyon proper lay before them. Canady grinned and wiped his streaming face.

It was hot, and going to get hotter.

"Hoss," he said, "they're pushing. They mean to take us. They must know the country ahead. They don't ride like there's any hurry."

The horse, now, did not respond with its ears and a turning of its soft eyes, as it had before. It stood, head-down, blowing out through its distended nostrils. Canady came back and squatted down and put his hand below the nose of the horse, where the moisture of its pained breathing would strike his palm.

"Damn," he said softly. "Blood."

He got his field glasses from the saddle pocket and examined the pursuers through them. "Eight," he said aloud, "and six ropes. I wonder how come it is that they always fetch so many ropes? Never saw a posse yet didn't feel that each of them ought to have a rope."

His fingers went to his sunburned neck. They felt it tenderly, and he grinned again. "Son of a gun," he said, "it could happen."

Canady's grins were not the grimaces of a fool, or of an unfeeling man. They were the grins of a gambler. And of an outlaw. And a thief. Canady knew where he was and where he had been and, most apparently, where he was going. It did not frighten him. He would grin when they put the loop over his head. That was his kind. He wouldn't curse or revile, and he wouldn't pray. Not out loud, anyway.

"Hoss," he said, "what do you think?"

The animal, slightly recovered, moved its ears and whickered gruntingly. Canady nodded, turning his back to the approaching posse and glassing the country ahead. "Me, too," he agreed. "A grunt and a whicker is all she's worth. We haven't got no place to go." He tensed, as he said it, the glasses freezing on an opening in the rearing base rock of the closing valley.

It was to their right. A good horse, fresh and sound, could take a man up to that gap in the cliff. The spill of detritus and an ages-old fan of boulders and stunted pine that lay below its lip would permit of perilous mounted passage. There was water up there, too, for Canady could see the small white ribbon of the stream splashing down a rainbow falls to mist upon the lower rocks in a spume of red and yellow and turquoise green lights, splendid with beauty in the early sun. "I take it back," he said. "Maybe we do have a place to go. Pretty, too, and handy to town. You can't beat that."

Directly ahead was a level sunlit flat, dotted with tall pines and scrub juniper and house-sized boulders. The clear stream from the high hole in the right-side valley wall watered the flat, growing good mountain hay upon its sandy red loam and making a ride across it a thing to pleasure the heart of any Western man.

"Come on," said Canady to his horse. "You canter me across the flat and I'll climb the fan afoot leaving you to pack up nothing but the saddle and the grub sack. You game? Least we can do is make those birds scratch for their breakfast. And who knows? Our luck might change. We might get up there and into that hole-in-the-wall before they come up to the rise, here, and spot us. If we can do that, there's a chance they'll ride on by, up the valley, and we can double back tonight and make it free."

He was talking to Canady, now, not to the horse. It was the way of men much alone when they needed to do some figuring. They would do it out loud, the way

31

Canady was doing. It sounded better that way, more convincing, and more as though it might really come off. Canady even swung into the saddle believing his own advice, telling himself what he wanted to know, then accepting it as a very good chance indeed. Again, it was his way. A man didn't live by the gun and the good fast horse without acquiring a working philosophy with lots of elastic in it.

"Move out," he repeated to the horse. "It's your part to get us across the flat in time."

The little mustang humped its back and shook itself like a wet dog. Running sweat, and caked as well, flew from its streaked hide. Its gathering of itself in response to the rider's words was a visible thing. The horse was like the man. It wouldn't quit short of the last second, or step, or shot. They were of a kind with the country around them. It was all the edge they had ever needed.

Canady panted. He wiped the perspiration from his eyes and started upward again. Behind him, the little horse came on, unled, the reins looped over the horn so as not to trail and be stepped on. He followed the man like a dog, panting with him, struggling where he struggled, sliding where he slid, and lunging on as he did, after each setback.

They had made it nearly to the top of the fan of fallen rock below and leading into the opening of the side canyon. In another four or five minutes they would be clear of the climb. They would be off the slide and safely into the notch in the high wall of the valley. They would be out of sight of the posse, and the posse still had not come into view of them on the rise back across the pine flat.

"Easy, hoss," gasped Canady. "We're going to make it."

But Canady was wrong. Thirty yards from the top, the mustang put its slender foreleg into a rock crevice and drew back quickly. The movement set the slide moving and caught the leg and crushed it like a matchstick below the knee. When the horse had freed itself and was standing hunched and trembling behind Canady, the shattered leg hung sickeningly a-swing and free of the ground, and Canady cursed with tears in his eyes. It was not the luck of it that brought his angry words, but the shame of it. It was his pity and his feeling for a gallant companion that had given its all and almost found it enough.

The hesitation, the wait there near the top of the slide, near the safety of the hole-in-the-wall, was the natural thing for a Western man. His horse was hurt. It was hopelessly hurt. He would have to leave it, but not like that. Not standing there on three legs hunched up in the middle with pain and fright. Not standing there watching him with those liquid brown eyes. No, he couldn't leave his horse like that.

But how else? He couldn't shoot the mustang, for the noise would key the posse to his location. Had he had a knife, he could cut its throat. Or had he an ax he could have crushed its skull above the eye socket and put the poor devil down painlessly. With a rock he might be able to stun the brave little brute, but he could not be sure of killing it cleanly. The same held true for the butt of his Colt or the steel-shod heel of his Winchester. He could stun the horse, likely put it to its knees, but not, still, be able to go on knowing it would not recover and would try to get up again and go on, and so suffer as no horse-riding man could think to let his mount suffer.

But, damn it, this was *his* life he was arguing with himself about. It wasn't the damned horse's life. If he didn't do something and do it quick, the posse would be over the rise and he and the horse could go to hell together. Well, he would use the Colt butt. He knew he could hit the exhausted animal hard enough with it to put it down for the necessary time for himself to get on into the hole-in-the-wall and for the posse to ride by and on up the valley. That was all the time he needed, or at least it was all he could ask for.

He pulled the Colt and started back to the horse, sliding and stumbling in his hurry to get to the trembling beast and knock it down. But when he got up to its side, when he looked into those dark eyes, he couldn't do it. He had to be sure.

"The hell with the posse," he said to the little horse, and spun the Colt in the air and caught it by the handle and put it behind the ragged ear and pulled the trigger. The smoke from the shot was still curling upward, and the little pony just going slowly down, when the first of the pursuing riders came up over the rise across the flat and yelled excitedly back to his comrades that the game was in sight, and on foot.

Canady went up the little stream. Behind him, where it fed the rainbow falls leaping outward into the main valley, the possemen were just topping the detritus fan and closing in on "the hole."

Back there Canady had made a decision. It was not to stay and fight from the entrance cleft of the hole, where the little rivulet went out of the side canyon. He did not know what lay on up the side canyon, and feared there

34

might be a way by which the possemen, familiar with this territory, could ride a circle and come in behind him. He could not risk that, he believed, and must go on up the creek as far as he could, hoping it would be far enough to find a place where he could put his back to the wall and fight without their being able to get behind him.

Now, going along, the way becoming steeper and narrower and the creek bank little more than wide enough to pass a good horse and rider, he saw ahead of him a basalt dike, or cross dam of rock, which cut across the narrowing floor of the side canyon. Here the stream took another plunge, this of about thirty feet. Above the dike, Canady could see the boles of pine trees and hence knew that the ground above the dike lay fairly level. The cross-laying of rock apparently served as a barrier against which the winter erosions of snow, ice and thaw had worked with the spring floodings of the creek to bring down soil and build up a tiny flat.

Canady's gray eyes lit up. His brown face relaxed and he said aloud, "By God, maybe this is it," and went on with renewed strength and some hope of keeping his life a little longer. Up there, above that rock cross-bank, a man with a good carbine and plenty of shells could hold down most eight-man posses for several afternoons. Well, two or three, anyway. Or one. For certain, until nightfall. Twelve, fifteen hours, say. It was better than nothing.

His luck held. There was a good angling trail going up that thirty-foot vertical face of rock. It was a game trail, and somewhat of a cow trail, too. He made out the droppings of elk, blacktail deer, range steers and, then suddenly and strangely, a fairly fresh piling of horse sign. This latter find sent a chill through him. He was on his knees in the instant of the sighting, but then he straightened, grinning. It was all right. The pony was unshod. Moreover, he suspected, from the hard round prints that it left, that it never had been shod and was one of a bunch of broomtails—wild mustangs—that came into this rocky depth for the water that flowed so green and cool in the stream.

Clearing the top of the stone dam, Canady's grin widened. The flat above lay precisely as he had imagined it did. He laughed softly, as a man will who is alone. Now, then, it would be a little different from the way those hungry lawmen had planned it. This was perfect. At the apex of the triangle of the flat he saw the thick stand of sycamore and cottonwood, aspen, laurel and willow, and he knew that the water headed there.

A moment later, he made out the source of the stream, a large artesian spring gushing from the native rock under great pressure. The spring was set above the grove some few feet, its stream falling rapidly to plunge into the foliage. Likely it pooled up there under the trees and at the foot of the down-plunge. That's what lured in the wild horses and the other game and the cattle, too, what few of the latter were hardy enough to come this far into the mountains for feed.

All a man would need to do now, was hole up in those boulders that girded the spring, up there above the trees, and he could command with his Winchester the whole of the small, open flat between the spring grove and the stone cross-dam that Canady had just clambered up.

Taking a deep breath, the fugitive started across the flat, toward the spring and its hole-up boulders. It was not until he had climbed safely into this haven at the canyon head and laid down pantingly to look back on his trail and get ready for the possemen, that he saw where he had come.

Below him in the trees the spring pooled up exactly as he had expected it would. Also the rim of the pool showed the centuries of wear of the hoofed animals coming to its banks for water. But there was something else—two other things—that he had not expected to see there, and his grin faded and his gray eyes grew taut and tired and empty.

The first thing was the wild horse. It had not gone on up out of the little side canyon as Canady had hoped, showing him the way to follow its tracks and escape over the rim where no mounted man might follow. It was still in the grove of trees that sheltered the spring-pool water-hole, and it wasn't still there because of its thirst.

Beyond the trees, back where Canady had come from, and so skillfully blended and built into the natural cover of the canyon that even his range-wise eyes had missed them, were the two woven brush and pole wings of the second thing Canady had not dreamed to find there. Those were the man-made wings of a mustang corral down there. Canady had stumbled into a wild-horse trap. And he was caught there, with this unfortunate lone mustang that now cowered in the trees and could not get out of the trap any more than could he, and for the same reason—the posse and the box canyon.

"Steady on," Canady called down softly to the terrified horse. "We'll think of something."

Two hours after high noon the sun was gone from the canyon. Canady could see its light splashing the far side of the main valley still, but in the side canyon all was soft shade, and hot. Canady drank enough water to keep himself from drying out, yet not enough to log him. He noted that the wild mustang did the same thing. It knew, as Canady knew, that to be ready to fight or fly called for an empty belly.

"Smart," said Canady, "smart as hell." The horse heard him and looked up. "*Coo-ee, coo-ee,*" Canady called to him reassuringly. "Don't fret; I'll figure something for us." But it was a lie and he knew it was a lie.

He had gone down, right after he first lay up in the spring boulders and saw the trap and the wild broomtail in it, and closed off the narrow gate of the funnel-winged corral with his lariat. He had done that in a hurry, before the posse had worked up into the canyon and taken its position along the top of the cross-dam. His one thought had been that the broomtail was a horse, wild or not, and that so long as a man had a horse he wasn't out of it in that country. And he had wanted to keep hidden from the posse the fact that he did have a horse up there in that headwaters' timber. The mustang had played with him in that last part of it, lying up shy and quiet as a deer in the trees and brush, not wanting any more than Canady wanted for the men to know that it was there.

"It" in this case was a scrubby little stallion, probably too small and old to hold a band of mares. The little horse had not only the fixtures but the temperament of the mongrel stud animal. Watching him lie still in the spring brush, his eyes following every move of the men below him, as well as of the single man above him, Canady knew that he and the trapped horse were friends. The only problem was proving it to the horse.

38

Sometimes these old scrub studs had been ridden long ago and would remember man's smell and voice. He tried a dozen times to talk the mustang up toward his end of the spring pool. But the animal gave no sign that the sight, scent or sound of mankind was familiar to him, or welcome. He bared his teeth silently and pinned his ears and squatted on his haunches ready to kick like a pack mule on a cold morning. He did this every time Canady said more than three or four words to him, or accompanied his talk with any movement that might mean he was coming down to see the horse, if the horse would not come up to see him.

What possible good the horse could do him, even if, by some miracle Canady might gentle him down and put his saddle and bridle on him, Canady didn't know. Then, even in thinking that far, he laughed and shrugged. His saddle and bridle were down there on that rock slide below the hole-in-the-wall. He'd had no time and no reason to take them off his dead mount. So if he went out of there astride that broomtail it would be bareback, and that was about as good a bet as that the crafty old stallion would sprout wings and fly up out of the canyon. A bridle, of sorts, he could rig from splitting and unraveling a short length of his lariat. It would be sort of a breaking hacka-more arrangement and might do to give simple directions of right and left and whoa-up.

But even if he rigged this Sioux headstall and got it on the shaggy little horse, then what? That was, even if the rascal wanted to be good, or had been ridden in the past, and remembered it of a sudden? Nothing. Not a damned thing. Canady couldn't ride out of that canyon if he had the best saddle mount in Montana waiting and eager to make the try with him. It was all crazy, thinking of that wild stud. But just finding any horse up there was bound to start a man's mind going. Especially when he had just shot his own mount and was fixing to put his back to the best rock he could find and go down with lead flying.

But it was crazy all the same. All Canady could do was what the old broomtail stud could do—fight the rope to the last breath he had in him, then kill himself, if he could, before the others did it for him.

The afternoon wore on. The heat in the deep-walled little canyon was enormous. The deerflies swarmed at the spring pool and bit like mad cats. They nearly drove Canady wild, but he fought them with hand and mind and swathed neckband and, when evening came, they lifted up out of the canyon on the first stir of the night wind.

In the early part of the waiting there had been some desultory talk between the posse and Canady, talk of Canady coming out peacefully and getting a fair trial, but the fugitive had not bothered to take that offer seriously. He knew the trial he would get. The posse had its own witnesses with it. They would bring up these two or three men who had "seen" the shooting and say to them, "Is that him?" and the men would say, "Yes, that's him," and the trial would be over. Witnesses! thought Canady. God, how he hated them.

It wasn't that he minded being identified if he was the man. In his business, no feeling was held against the witness who *had* seen something. It was those devils, like the ones with the posse, who had *not* seen the job and yet who were always ready to raise their right hands and be sworn, who were the ones Canady hated.

There had not been any witnesses to what passed between him and that teller. All the other bank people had been on the floor behind the cage, and there had been no customers in the bank, or out in front of it. The shooting had happened and Canady had made it to his horse in back of the bank, and made it away down the alley and into the sagebrush south of town before he had passed a living soul. Then, it was two farm wagons, both carrying kids and driven by women, that he had ridden by well out of Gray's Landing. How those good folks—and they were the only real witnesses, save the cashier and the other teller on the bank floor—how they could identify him as anything other than a horseman not of that area, Canady did not know.

As for the three shots that had killed the teller, and they must have killed him or the posse would not have pushed so hard, those shots had been fired *after* both barrels of the .36 caliber derringer that the teller brought up out of the cash drawer had been triggered and put their slugs, one in Canady's chest, and one in the ceiling of the Second National Bank of Gray's Landing, Montana.

But the only witness to that fact was dead. Canady had reacted as all men with guns in their hands react to other men with guns in their hands. He had fired by instinct, by pure conditioned reflex of long experience, when that first .36 bullet went into the pectoral muscles of his left chest.

Armed robbery? Certainly. Twenty years in the Territorial Prison? Of course. A man expected that. But to be run down like a mad dog and cornered and starved out and then strung up on a naked cottonwood like a damned Indian drunk or a common horse thief was not right or fair. Murder? Could you call it murder when the other man was a professional in his business and he could see that you were a professional in yours? When you told him he would be killed if he tried anything funny? Then, when on top of the fair warning, you gave him the first shot? Could you call it murder, then, if you shot in answer to his try at killing you? Self-defense was the actual verdict, but of course an armed robber could not plead self-defense. But he was not guilty of murder, or even of assault with a deadly weapon, or even of intent to commit murder, or of a damned thing, really, but to sack that cash drawer and clear out of Gray's Landing just as fast and peaceably as he and the old horse might manage.

Canady grinned, even as he exonerated himself.

It was no good. He knew it was no good. A man had to be honest with himself. If he was in another business he wouldn't need a gun to conduct his trade. Needing and using a gun, he was always in the peril of being forced to use it. The teller was an honest man. Frank Canady was a crook. The teller was a dead honest man, and Canady was a live dishonest man. Canady was a killer.

"No!" he yelled down to the posse. "I won't do it; I shot second; I didn't mean to harm that fellow. He pulled on me and shot first. But he's dead, ain't he? Sure he is. And you say to me to come on down peaceable and you'll see I get a fair trial? With a dead teller back there on the floor of the Second National? That's rich. Really rich."

The possemen were startled. It had been two hours since the fugitive had made a sound. Previously he had refused to come down and they had thought he meant it. Now, did they detect a change? Was it that he wanted to reconsider and was only protecting his ego by the defiant

42

outburst? What was all this about?

"That's right, you heard us right," the leader of the posse called up to him. "You come down here and we'll guarantee to take you back to Gray's Landing and get you to either Cheyenne or Miles City, wherever the court is sitting, by train and under armed guard. You'll get the trial we promised, and the protection beforehand." He waited a significant moment, then demanded, "What do you say? There's no use any more people getting hurt."

Canady's gray eyes grew tired again.

"That's so," he called back. "It includes me, too. I don't want to see anybody else get it, either. 'Specially me. No thanks, Mr. Posseman. I'll stay up here. I don't fancy that you brung along all them ropes just to tie me up for the ride back to Gray's Landing."

There was a silence from below the cross-dam of rock in the upper throat of the canyon that lasted perhaps two, perhaps three stretching minutes. Then the posseman called back.

"All right," he said, "you'll have it your way. When it's full dark we're going to come for you, and you know what that will mean. There are eight of us, all good shots, and you won't have the chance of a rat in an oat bin. We've got bull's-eye lanterns to light you out. We will set them up behind boulders where you can't snipe them, and yet where they will throw light up there around you like it was bright moonlight. We mean to stomp you out. There will be no trial and no talk of a trial. You're dead right now."

Canady sank back behind his breastwork of basalt and gray-green granite. He hawked the cottony spittle from his throat and spat grimacingly down toward the mustang stud. The animal had been crouching and listening to the exchange of voices intelligently like some big gaunt sandy-maned dog. Seeing him, and noting his apparent interest, Canady managed a trace of his quiet grin.

"What do *you* say, *amigo?*" he asked.

The horse looked up at him. It was the first time in all the long hours that Canady had tried gentle-talking to him that the animal had made a direct and not spooked response to the man's voice. Now he stomped a splayed and rock-split forehoof and whickered softly and gruntingly in his throat, precisely as Canady's old horse had done.

"All right," said Canady, for some reason feeling mightily warmed by the mustang's action, "so we've each got one friend in the world. That isn't too bad. As long as you have a friend you have a chance. Rest easy; let me think. We'll still make it, you and me. . . ."

It was dusk when the old steer came down the cliff trail. He was a ladino, one of those mossy-horned old rascals that had successfully hidden out from the gathers of a dozen years. He was old and crafty and cautious as any wild animal, but he had to have water and he was coming down to the spring pool to get it.

He certainly saw the men of the posse, and winded their mounts, but they did not see him and he knew that they did not. His yellow buckskin hide with the dark *"cruz"* or cross-stripe on the shoulders, and the dark brown legs and feet, blended perfectly into the weathered face of the cliff, and he made no more sound coming down that hidden trail than a mountain doe might have made. But he had failed to see Canady or to separate his scent,

44

or the scent of the mustang stud, from the other horse and man scents coming from below.

He came on, carefully, silently, yet quickly down the wall of the canyon from the rim above and Canady, seeing him, was suddenly lifted in mind and heart. He had been right in the first place! There *was* a trail up out of that blind box of a side canyon. A track up that dizzy sheer cliff, up there, that would pass a desperate man, or a catlike wild mustang, but not a mounted man or a man going afoot leading his tamed and trained saddle mount.

"Come on, come on," he heard himself whispering to the old outlaw steer. "Come on down here and let me see how you do it. Let me see how and where you get off that damned wall and down here where we are."

He grinned when he said that, when he said "we," meaning himself and the wild stud, without thinking about it. It was funny how a man took to anything for a friend when he had run out of the real McCoy and was in his last corner. He supposed that if a sidewinder crawled along at the final minute and that was all he had to talk to, a man would find some excuse to think kindly of the snake tribe. Well, anyway, he was thinking with deep kindness about the animal kingdom just then. Especially the horse and cow part of it. And extraspecially about the latter half.

"Come on, keep coming on, don't slip, for God's sake," he said to the gaunt dun steer. "Easy, easy. Let me see you do it, just don't fall or spook or get a bad smell and change your mind. That's it, that's it. Easy, easy. . . ."

He talked the steer down that cliff trail as though his life depended on it, and it did. And the steer made it. He made it in a way that caused Canady to suck in his breath and shake his head in wonderment. He made it in a way that even caused Canady to think for a moment about there being something to the idea of a divine providence, for it was the sort of thing no man could have figured out by himself, the weird, crazy, wonderful kind of a last-second reprieve that no force but God Almighty could have sent to a man in Canady's place. It was a miracle.

The dun steer performed it with an easy quickness that defied belief, too. He came to that place on his side of the canyon where it seemed to Canady that the trail must end. The man could see the sheer face of the rock dropping sixty feet to the creek bed. A giant outcropping of granite hid the exact end of the right-side trail, but Canady could see, and with absolute certainty, that the trail did not continue downward past that outcrop that hid its actual terminus.

But as he watched the steer disappear behind the outcrop and as he wondered what would happen next, he saw the lean yellow body lurch itself in a graceful leap from behind the outer edge of the outcrop, and sail outward through the thin air of the canyon's dark throat. It appeared as though the leap would smash the ribby brute into the rearing face of the opposite, left-hand canyon wall, which lay no more than fifteen or twenty feet from the right-side wall. But again the steer disappeared, this time seemingly into the very face of the opposing cliff.

There was a tricky turn in the rock wall of the canyon's left side at just that point, however, and while Canady could see the creek's raggedly broken bottom, he could not see where the steer hit into the wall. All he was sure of for the moment was that the animal had made his landing somewhere other than in the creek bottom. Diffi-

cult as it might be to accept, that old outlaw steer had somehow made it from one side of the wall to the other. But, even so, then what? Where was he now? The questions were soon answered when the missing steer appeared to walk right out of the waterfall that came down from Canady's elevated vantage to strike into and begin following the brief section of creek bed into the pool grove. While Canady gaped, the animal stole swiftly to the pool, drank sparingly, returned and disappeared again behind the curtain of misty water cascading down from the spring above.

So that was it. As simple and as remarkable as that. A trail ran from behind the waterfall up the left-hand wall. At a point opposite the right-side trail's end, it, too, terminated. But it was obvious that there was room enough for a running jump and opposite safe landing, to and from either wall, with both takeoff and landing spots completely masked from the lower canyon.

Gauging the distance of the jump, Canady knew that he could make it. With his boots off and laced about his neck, or better, thrown over with his Colt and the saddlebags with the bank money, the Winchester being slung on his back, alone, he could make that distance through the air. But, then, what of that? He made the jump safely and went on up the right-side cliff trail behind the ladino steer and gained the rim; then what? He would still be afoot in a hostile land in midsummer's blazing heat without food, water, or a mount.

That was the rub. Even if he made that jump and the cliff climb beyond it and got to the rim, he would have to have a horse. Otherwise, the possemen, within an hour or two of dark, having come for him and found him gone, would go back out and climb out of the main valley and cut for his sign on both rims of the side canyon, and they would still get him. They would get him, easy, with them mounted and him afoot.

No, he had to take that broomy studhorse with him.

Somehow, he had to get that mustang to go with him up the cliff. If he could do that, could get the little horse to make the jump with him on its back—it would have to be that way for he could never trust the brute to follow him or to wait for him if he allowed it to jump first—if he could make that gap in the canyon on the back of that little wild horse, then stay with him, hand-leading him up the cliff trail, then, oh then, by the dear good Lord, he would make it. He and the horse would make it together. Just as he had promised the raunchy little devil. Up on the rim, he would remount the tough wiry mustang and together they would race away and Canady would have his life and the broomtail stud would have his freedom and the Gray's Landing posse would have their ropes unstretched and their vengeance unadministered and left to God where it belonged.

The thought of the Almighty came very strong to Canady in that moment of desperate hope. He turned his face upward to peer out of the narrow slit of late twilight far above him where the walls of the canyon seemed almost to touch at the top and where, far, far up there, he could now see the yellow steer climbing the last few steps of the steep trail and humping himself over the rim and losing himself to canyon's view.

Canady nodded and said to the dusk-hushed stillness about him: "If you'll let me make it, too, Lord, me and that little hoss down yonder, Lord, the bank don't need it and I won't want it any more after this night, and I will give this money to the widow of that poor teller. I will figure some way to do it, Lord, that she don't know where it came from. And I'll turn loose this little wild hoss, if you will let me gentle him enough to get on him and push him to that jump, up yonder. I'm going to try it, Lord. I'm going down there to the pool and try putting my loop on him right now. You reckon you could help me? I surely hope so, as I think you wouldn't send that ladino steer down here to show a man the way out, and then not help him to make it. Nor likewise do I think you would put that little old mustang studhorse down there in that trap by the pool unless you wanted him used. It looks to me, Lord, as if you truly wanted to pull me out of this here trap, and if that's the way it is, why thank you and I'll do my best. . . ."

In the little light remaining, Canady went down from his rocks by the spring to try for the trapped wild horse. He took his rope from the trap gate and closed the gate, instead, with brush and poles, hoping it would turn the stud should he break past him when he came at him with the lariat.

The actual catching went, as such things perversely will, with a strange easiness. Oh, the little horse fought the loop when he felt it settle on him, but he did not do so viciously. The very fact that he permitted Canady to come close enough to dab the loop on him to begin with was peculiarly simple.

It made the matter suspicious to Canady and he thought the little stud was merely stalling on him, was trying to tempt him in close where he could use his teeth and hooves on him. He knew the small mustangs would do this. They would fight like panthers in close, using their teeth like carnivorous animals, and their feet with all the savagery of elk or moose fighting off wolves.

But this was not the case with the tattered broomtail in the mustang trap. When Canady got up near enough to him, he saw the reason why, or thought that he did. The telltale white marks of the cinch and saddle, the places where white hair had grown in to replace the original claybank sorrel hairs, showed clearly in the darkening twilight. Canady's first thought that this horse had been handled before was now assured. And it certainly explained the change in the animal the moment the man snugged the loop high up on his neck, under the jaw, in a way that showed the horse he meant to hold him hard and fast, and to handle him again as he had been handled years before. Memory is a strong force.

The stud made Canady throw him on the ground, using the loose end of the rope to make a figure-8 snake and roll it around the front legs to bring the little pony down, but once he had been thrown and permitted to stand up again, it was all over. This man had gentled many horses. He had spent his life with them. Their smell had become his smell. The very sound of his voice had a horse sound in it. The mustang had heard it in the man's first words. He had sensed his kinship with this particular man, then, and he sensed his mastery of horsekind, now. He submitted to Canady and stood quietly, if still trembling, while the man stroked him and sweet-whispered to him and got him to ease and to stand without shaking, and without dread or apprehension.

Then Canady cut and wove the makeshift breaking

52

halter, the Plains Indians' simple rope rein and bridle arrangement, continuing to talk all the while to the small mustang. When, in half an hour more, it was full dark and the split-ear hackamore-bridle and its short reining rope were finished and put upon the horse, the animal was to all practical purposes reduced to a usable saddle horse.

It was a piece of the greatest luck, Canady knew, that he had been able to catch and work the little brute. But it was not so entirely luck that it had no sense or possibility to it, and his success only made the fugitive believe that his hunch of higher help was a true one, and this thought, in turn, strengthened him and made his spirits rise.

"Come on," he murmured to the little horse, "It's time we got out of here. Come along, *coo-ee, coo-ee,* little hoss. That's good, that's real good. Easy, easy. . . ."

They went in behind the creek falls, as the yellow ladino steer had done. The mustang pulled back a bit at the water, but once it had hit him he steadied down and followed Canady's urging pull on the lariat as well and as obediently as any horse would have done in similar straits. Beyond the sheet of the falls, the left-hand trail went sharply but safely upward and around the trunklike bulge of the canyon's wall which had hidden it from Canady's view at the spring. Around the turn was the expected straight run at the leap-over.

It was better, even, than Canady hoped. There was some actual soil in its track and, here and there, some clumps of tough wire grass to give footing and power for the jump.

"Steady, now," said Canady, and eased up onto the crouching mustang. The little mount flinched and deepened his crouch, but he did not break. Canady sighed gratefully and nodded upward to that power which clearly was helping him now. He took his grip on the rope rein and put the pressure of his bowed knees to the mustang's ribs. Beneath him, he felt the little horse squat and gather himself. Then he touched him, just touched him, with his left bootheel. The wild stud uncoiled his tensed muscles, shot down the runway of the trail, came up to the jump-across as though he had been trained to it since colthood.

Canady felt his heart soar with the mighty upward spring in the small brute's wiry limbs. He laughed with the sheer joy of it. He couldn't help it. He had never in his life felt a triumph such as this one; this sailing over that hell's pit of blackness down there beneath him; this gliding spring, this arching, floating burst of power that was carrying him high above those deadly rock fangs so far below, and was carrying him, too, up and away from those blood-hungry possemen and their winking, glaring, prying bull's-eye lanterns, which he could just see now, from an eye-corner, coming into view down-canyon of his deserted place at the spring above the pool and the peaceful grove of mountain ash and alder and willow there at the head of Rainbow Creek in Blind Canyon, sixty and more miles from the Second National Bank and that fool of a dead teller in Gray's Landing, Montana.

Oh, what a wondrous, heady thing was life! And, oh! what a beholden and humble man was Frank Canady for this gift, this chance, this answer to his fumbling prayer. He would never forget it. Never, never, never.

They came down very hard at the far end of the jump. The concussion of the horse hitting the ground rattled Canady's teeth and cracked his jaws together as loud as a pistol shot. He saw lights behind his eyes and heard wild and strange sounds, but only for a second or two. Then all was clear again and he and the little horse were going together up the right-side cliff trail, Canady leading the way, the little horse following faithfully as a pet dog behind him. It seemed no more than a minute before they were where it had taken the yellow steer half an hour to climb, and it seemed only a breath later that they had topped out on the rim and were free.

Canady cried then. The tears came to his eyes and he could not help himself. He didn't think that the little mustang would care, though, and he was right. When he put his arms about the shaggy, warm neck and hugged the skinny old stud, the mustang only whickered deep in his throat and leaned into Frank Canady and rested his homely jughead over the man's shoulder. They were of a kind. They belonged to each other, and with each other, and that was true; for that was the way that the possemen found them when they came probing carefully up the bed of the creek in its brief run from the deserted pool grove to the foot of the waterfall.

The horse had fallen with the man beneath him, and neither had known a flash or a spark or a hint of thought in the instant their lives had been crushed out among the granite snags of the creek bed below the jumping place of the yellow ladino steer.

THE WHITE RIDERS

By Glenn R. Vernam

I guess I am the only living link with what actually happened to old Cholla Davis, or what he thought happened; the only one to hear the details of his meeting with the White Riders. Of course, the main part about him and Bill Rickey being stranded out in the desert without water, was more or less familiar to most of the old-timers around that part of the country. The two of them had been across into Mexico and were returning over the old Diablo Trail when their luck ran out. That was long before my time, while Cholla was still crawling up toward voting age, but various people had kept the story alive. I first heard it from one of the Drag-8 hands. It was this fellow and his partner who found them out on a sand flat. Rickey was dead, and Cholla had certainly got to where he could look over into the other world, if such a thing is possible. What he saw there, however, was something else again, something nobody else ever knew, not even me, until that last night.

I haven't done any talking, either, since that night. I was just a button at the time, with the natural reactions of a lone kid in a grown-up outfit, scared of being laughed at or accused of grazing on loco stems. Later years and the usual string of acquaintances offered me little encouragement to sound off about such an off-center occurrence. So the story still stands as old Cholla finally unloaded it that night down on the Gila. But it's as clear as if it were yesterday. I can still hear his low, thin voice and see him sitting over across the campfire, the flickering firelight making phantom-like shadows across his caved-in cheeks and his eyes holding on to whatever he was watching out there in the empty darkness. I guess seeing him tell it had as much as anything to do with giving it reality; that, and what happened shortly afterward.

I had only known Cholla a couple of months. He had been line riding for the Rafter Bar when I drifted down into Squaw Valley and hooked on as an extra hand. Being a maverick kid and lonesome for any pat on the head made me a natural for his easy friendliness and his habit of siding with me whenever things got a little scaly. Why he took a liking to me I'll never know. I just accepted it and rode with him most of the time. We made sort of an odd pair. I was still in the fuzzy stage and slabby as a new colt, while he looked as old as the hills. I don't suppose he was actually over forty-five or fifty, but the tired old eyes under straggly wisps of snow-white hair, and the skinny frame humped over like it labored him to pack his scant hundred and forty pounds, would have fit a man of seventy. The boys said he had looked that way ever since his battle with the desert. However, I never gave much thought to his age. He was just old Cholla, and the way he eased range savvy into my thick skull without rawhiding my already badly bruised ego was all that counted in my book.

This particular day, we had been stray-hunting in an ornery, upended stretch of country over along the Gila. Night found us camped down by the river, with our day's gathering bedded down in a swale that angled back against the bluff. It had been a hard day. That sort of country is a tough proposition any way you take it. Moreover, Cholla's horse had taken a fall during the afternoon, shaking him up considerably. He had cracked his head against a rock and was looking pretty well faded by the time we made camp. He claimed the hurt was wearing off, though, and a night's rest would straighten him out all right. I naturally let it go at that. Such mishaps are everyday stuff in cow work.

Still, as the evening wore on I got the feeling of something queer about his actions—just little things. You know how you will usually spot any stray off-note in a close friend without being exactly able to put your finger on it. With him, it was sort of a fidgety restlessness instead of his usual quiet manner, and there was an odd kind of a far-off look in his eyes when he thought I wasn't noticing. He seemed eager to talk, which was never his way. He even went so far as to volunteer some of his early-day experiences down along the border, a thing I'd never known him to do before.

It must have been crowding nine o'clock when he broke off in the middle of a yarn about some Yaqui outlaws and a white settler's wife. I remember I was still humped over, shoving some greasewood chunks into the fire at the time. His sudden silence was like someone had jerked a door shut between us. I could actually feel the quiet settle down like a heavy blanket, the way it does ahead of a storm or just before a spooked herd breaks. A funny cold breath seemed to crawl up along my withers as I twisted around to see what had stopped him.

Cholla was still propped up against his saddle, like he'd been for the past hour. But I saw at once that he wasn't paying any attention to me; his eyes were centered off in the darkness beyond camp. One side of his face was half turned toward the firelight's jumpy glow, while his head was canted sidewise as if he were listening for something. Another chilly streak rippled up in the direction of my shirt collar and started a question toward my lips. Cholla, however, turned his face back at that instant, and it was his question that set me back on my heels a second time.

"I never told you about that time the desert rawhided Bill Rickey and me, did I?" he asked, in the tone of a man wanting to unload something and not quite knowing how to begin.

I just sat there staring out over my open mouth for a moment. I knew from experience how getting him to talk about that particular subject was like butting your head against a rocked-up doorway. Now, I managed to choke back my surprise enough to blurt out "No."

He slowly twisted up a smoke, half turning once more to stare off into the night, while I dug for words that might help him get started. This was something I'd been wanting to hear for a long time, and my scattered wits were slowly closing in on the idea that this was my big chance.

"That must have been one tough trip," I finally got out by way of encouragement. "Lucky it didn't finish you like it did Rickey."

"There was no luck about it!" His sharp reply hauled me up short with my mouth still hanging open. Then he went on slow and thoughtful, as though dragging memory up bit by bit to find the words: "No, luck had no hand in it. I wanted to go with Bill, begged 'em to take me, but they claimed my name wasn't on the books. I'd just have to bide my time, they said."

"They?" I barked, jerking up like a shot-stung wolf. "Who are they? What do you mean?"

"The White Riders." His voice had turned kind of low and toneless, with little pauses between the words. "The bunch that come for Rickey." And I saw his eyes swing around for another peek at whatever he'd been studying out there in the darkness.

The feel of it is kind of hard to put into words, and I only wish I could picture the whole setting as it was that night. Overhead, the big, white, fire-bright stars blazed down out of a purple-black sky, almost within reach, as if lighting the way for the half-pie of moon already climbing up over the ridge to the east. The old river at our feet seemed to be growling muffled answers to the breeze whispering in off the desert. Sounds of sleepy cattle bedded down in the swale added stealthy footlike rustlings to the soft tinkle of our horse bells out in the darkness. And there, as sort of a centerpiece for it all, the little circle of campfire light flickered back and forth throwing phantom shadows around Cholla's gaunt body and mummy-like features. I was still trying to make my hat hold my short hair down when his hollow-eyed face turned back in my direction and his cigarette butt spun into the fire.

"I've never found your mind exactly hidebound," he said, settling back into position. "Maybe it'll stretch over this deal. Most people couldn't savvy it. I don't myself, entirely. But it was all there. And 'twas something outside the range o' luck."

Cholla slid further down against the saddle as he sketched over the first part of the story. He knew I'd already heard the main points of it. He just filled in some of the details about how he and Rickey decided to take the chancy Diablo Trail instead of going the longer way around. Both were young and strong and good desert men. They never gave the idea of trouble any thought. And they would have likely made out all right if they hadn't run into a sandstorm that tied them up for two days out in the middle of that hell-bounded stretch of sand and rock.

The storm left them worn to a whisper, with grub gone and canteens all but empty. One horse had pulled his picket pin to drift with the wind, while the other was half dead from thirst and breathing so much sand. There was nothing they could do but try to reach a doubtful waterhole they knew about. Waterholes were scarce as gamblers at a prayer meeting. They tried to take the remaining horse along, but the poor critter laid down for the last time a little past noon, just after they had emptied their last canteen. It was just as well. Early the next day they found the waterhole full of sand and dry as a bone.

I shoved a couple of chunks up into the fire, slow and easylike with one foot, while he rambled along in a dreamy sort of a way that sounded more like he was talking to himself about something nobody else could understand. I caught myself half holding my breath to hear better.

That dry hole was a right sorry disappointment (Cholla's low voice went on). We'd already been nigh on t'eighteen hours without grub or water, and the heat had started our eyes playin' tricks. We straightened up to face north across the desert where we knowed the Drag-8 ranch ran down out of some green hills up along the border. It was a long ways; we didn't dare think how far. But it was our only chance. Nobody needed to say nothin'. We just hitched up our pants an' struck out.

My mem'ry ain't right clear after that day. What with the heat and no water we came unraveled pretty fast. I know we stopped to rest a couple times. We shore needed it. The last time was just after sundown. But it seemed like we hadn't more'n got bedded down when another brassy hot sun started proddin' at us. After that, it's all a blur—blazin' sky and red-hot sand and an endless stretch of shovin' one hoof ahead of t'other.

I r'member pilin' my gun and most of my clo'es under a greasewood sometime. And once I started lopin' out 'cross country towards a pretty little crick all lined with wavin' green trees—seemed I could even hear the water tricklin' over the rocks. But Bill snagged onto me an' helt me down till the scenery came to its normal self—nekked ground and a red-gold sun and the hot blue sky, with nothin' but heat waves and a pair o' buzzards floatin' in between. Them buzzards bothered me most, I 'member. All I could think of was the way they'd allus hang around over sick or crippled critters out on the range.

I never mentioned that stuff to Bill, though. He was havin' trouble enough as 'twas. Anyhow, my tongue had got so big by that time that 'twas hard t' talk. And all the while that mis'able sun kept pushin' down on my skull till my head felt plumb flat. My legs got to where they felt like two dead sticks, and the hot sand fairly blistered my feet as I dragged 'em up and set 'em down. I'd throwed my boots away somewheres along the line.

From time to time we kept seein' other streams an' ponds. One was a lake lookin' fer all the world like a young ocean. It took everythin' we had to keep each other from runnin' hisself ragged tryin' to reach 'em. In spite of knowin' desert mirages, it was hard to believe. I don't reckon one man alone could 'a' kept from sidewheelin' off in all directions. I know it took nigh all the reason both of us had left to p'vent first one, then t'other of us from goin' haywire.

But we did keep movin', somehow. I don't know if 'twas just that day an' the next, or two days and nights and part of the third. It might even been longer for all I could say. There was a few dark spells, I r'member, but they might 'a' been some of the times when I caved in. All the rest was hours an' hours of blazin' sun. It seemed like ten years. But a man's mind an' judgment gets tol'able snarled at times like that. I couldn't rightly say just how long it was.

Anyhow, the sun was near the horizon when I keeled over the last time. I thought it was evenin', but I might 'a' had my directions mixed. Bill tried to get me back on my feet, but he was too far gone hisself to do much. We were both on our knees, pawin' each other like a pair o' drunks, when we tumbled over sidewise and sprawled apart. Neither of us had the stren'th to try any further. My last recollection was hopin' I didn't look as much like a corpse as Bill did, even though I sure felt like one.

He was a plumb sorry sight. His tongue was swelled half out of his mouth and his cracked lips was all black with alkali and dried blood. His eyes looked like a pair of big red holes in an old skull, and I could see the shape of his ribs through his blistered old hide where his shirt was gone. I turned my eyes away for a bit. It looked to me like the ground an' sun had tangled themselves up in a mess of rainbow streaks shootin' out of a black velvet curtain.

I reckon I was plenty rocky myself. I seemed to be all one big burnin' misery. But 'twasn't long 'fore them colored streaks petered out and the black curtain slapped down over ever'thin'.

The next thing I knowed was coming to all of a sudden. I felt like something had roused me. I distinctly recall rollin' over and settin' up. It seemed as bright as day, though I can't r'member seein' any sun, and the air was just comf'tably warmish. My hurtin' had all faded out into a sort of lazy tiredness, like comes on a Sunday mornin' after a big night in town. I could see the hills over where the Drag-8 lay, not more'n six, eight miles off, and the dry country stretchin' out in the other direction. Bill was already awake, sittin' up over to my left. I noticed he was starin' off towards the west, like as if he was watchin' somethin'.

I must 'a' set there a couple minutes, gettin' my bearin's. Ever'thin' was clear as you'd ever see it and I was wide awake as I am now. Then I heard it ag'in, the noise that had woke me. I twisted 'round in the direction of Bill's gaze.

'Twas then I saw 'em. Ten or a dozen riders was

headed our way at a stiff lope. They looked mighty pretty, far off as they were, bobbin' against the skyline. And they was singin' some kind of a song. That was what woke me. I never could recall the words later, though they seemed plain enough then. Mem'ry of it makes me think of three, four old range songs shuffled in with some hymns to make a full deck. Sweet an' movin' it was, though, all accomp'nied by soft, low music that seemed to be comin' from the jinglin' of their spurs 'n' bit-chains.

As they come closer I saw they was all ridin' milk-white hosses with white outfits to match. Saddles, chaps, clo'es and all was the same color. Their bits an' spurs looked to be polished silver. So was their stirrups and other metal trimmin's. Handsome was no name for it!

And here's another odd thing : While I was watchin' them, I had no feelin' of bein' scared or spooked up, like a man ordinarily would feel at sight of such an unusual outfit. Ever'thin' seemed plumb natural and accordin' to Hoyle. All I felt was some normal curiosity and a heap of pleasure seein' such a sightly bunch.

While they was still about a hundred yards off, the party kinda fanned out, and I could see one of the boys in the center was leadin' an extra hoss. It was all saddled an' bridled and a roll o' white clothes was tied behind the cantle and white chaps hung across the horn. I r'member the first thing that struck me was wonderin' why they hadn't brung two. It seemed plumb natural they should be comin' for us.

A minute later they swung around in a half circle to pull up right near where Bill was sittin'. I'd half noticed a cool breeze blowin' in from their direction as they rode along. Now it seemed to be sorta suckin' around us in whirlwind fashion. 'Tweren't rightly cold; just cool and damp. Something like a man would feel standin' in the mouth of a cave or under a wet sheet on a hot day.

As soon as they stop, the gent with the extra hoss pulls over alongside Bill. For maybe a dozen seconds he sits there sizin' things up. Then he steps down and lifts Bill to his feet. A minute later, he begins helpin' him into that white outfit. I can still see how tickled Bill looked.

Nobody paid no attention to me. I stood it as long as I could, then let out a holler in their direction. I didn't hanker to be overlooked. But not a one of 'em batted an eye my way. It was just like I didn't exist. I hollered an' waved some more—same results. I even tried to call Bill's attention by gettin' real personal. That didn't help none, neither.

I was beginnin' to feel plumb hostile by then. I saw no call for him to high-hat me thataway, just 'cause some tony outfit had picked him up. I was fairly hotheaded, anyhow, them days. I finally started over there to do somethin' about it. I aimed to let him know he couldn't get shut o' me without an argument.

But I didn't get very far. I was weak as a new calf. In spite of feelin' so good, I couldn't do much but weave an' wobble when I got on my feet.

Still, I hadn't staggered more'n just a few steps 'fore the boss of the outfit, or what I took to be the boss, looked my way kind of appraisin'-like. I hurried the best I could, but hadn't covered more'n half my length when he shook his head crosswise an' motioned me back. I tried to ask him what he had ag'in my comp'ny, and kept comin'.

When I saw Bill step into the saddle and ever'body start gatherin' up their reins, I got desp'rate and tried to run. But I couldn't hack it. My feet wouldn't behave. About the second jump, my legs buckled sidewise and my face plowed into the sand. Then I tried crawlin'—without much better luck. I could just barely move.

About then, the bunch began reinin' around and settlin' themselves in their saddles. I saw they was set to pull out. I guess I took on a fright, howlin' and beggin' not to be left there. My commotion finally caused the boss to turn back and look me over real long and careful. Then he shook his head some more and spoke for the first time.

I couldn't go this trip, he explained. There was nothing personal or uncompliment'ry about it; it just had to be played accordin' to the rules. When my card turned up, they'd be back after me. Meanwhile, I stayed on the ground.

Well, I bawled an' begged a lot more, but 'tweren't no good. With a wave of his hand, he swung back into the head of the outfit and the whole bunch started movin' off with Bill in the middle. A minute later, they was headed back towards the west, lopin' along in a big white cloud of flyin' manes an' tails and bobbin' riders. And they was singin' that song ag'in in a way that'd bust your heart.

I just laid there too miser'ble to lift my head, watchin' 'em get smaller an' smaller while their singin' died down to a scant whisper. The cool breeze had left with them, leavin' it hotter'n ever. I was hurtin' all over ag'in, only worse. Felt like I was in a tight Dutch-oven banked with red-hot coals. Fire streaks started gougin' up into my eyeballs and on through the top of my head. Then ever'thin' went black.

The next thing I knowed was wakin' up in the Drag-8 bunkhouse, tryin' to suck water out of a medicine dropper. I was a plumb wreck. Alive was about all you could say for me. The boss told me how a couple of his hands had noticed some circlin' buzzards and rode out on the flat t' investigate. They found Bill stiff as a ramrod and me little better. Said I was layin' sprawled face down at the end of a string of tracks, where I'd staggered an' crawled towards Bill's body. They claimed it looked . . . looked like I'd been . . . try . . . i . . n . . n. . . . .

Cholla's voice trailed off in sort of a thin whisper as his head rocked sideways a trifle and then fell forward on his chest.

Dead? Sure he was dead! The coroner's verdict, later, was "Instantaneous death from a blood clot on the brain." It was explained to everybody's satisfaction by the bump on his head where the horse threw him against that rock.

But here's the part that still makes me take a good long look at myself every so often: I had been so bogged down in what Cholla had been telling that it took me a few moments to shake myself back to reality. When I finally wrangled my wits into action and got around on the other side of the fire, he was sagged down against his saddle, one thumb still hooked in his belt. While I stood there, wondering what to do next, I heard a low humming noise in the air. It struck me then, and still hangs in my memory, as the sound of singing off in the distance. It had a sort of sweet melody. A moment later, I snapped up with a jerk as a bit-chain rattled suddenly close behind me. I'd have sworn it was a bit-chain, yet when I turned around, there was nothing there. About the same moment, a chill, dampish breeze set in from across the river. It blew steadily for a bit, then swirled around like a baby whirlwind and disappeared as suddenly as it had come.

I looked down again at Cholla. As I straightened him out on a saddle blanket, I couldn't help noticing how his face had smoothed out. He actually looked years younger, with his lips relaxed like a baby asleep, sort of contented and smiling. And as the breeze died down, my ears caught that low humming again, growing fainter as it faded away in the distance.

BACK BEFORE THE MOON

By S. Omar Barker

On a little meadow slope of the Hidden Valley that lies behind the black woods of the Upper Vallecitos stands a great cross built of red stone. This is in the Rio Arriba country of New Mexico, where all the world is still outside, and where there are said to be strange sights every night of a moon for those with eyes to see them. Here, then, is how the red stone cross came to be. If you had seen it you would want to know. And old Oliborio Baldonado, the graybeard, squatting in the sun beside his adobe in Cañoncito, would tell you, as he told me:

Eligio Jaramillo came riding down out of the black woods from the Valle Escondido, and all the little *cañons* ran belly-deep in snow-water to stop him. The river itself, modest and clear-eyed in summer, now boomed through its red stone box like the wrath of *Mi Tata Dios,* and then swung violently into the three-cornered cove where Eligio would have to cross it.

Without warning, a great pine came swooping down across his path; his pony reared and swung around in futile struggle back up the hill. Eligio's eyes widened in sudden alarm. Then the deeper fear that drove him down the sweeping slopes of the mountains returned to his eyes. He jerked his *caballito* back down the hill, spurred him to flounder around the fallen tree and on again, down the slippery trail to the river, which snaked down the steep *cañon* in coils ten feet deep and fifty feet from edge to edge. He could not hope to cross the river, yet he would have to.

Back in the squat cabin with a flat dirt roof, on a long grass slope tipped up to the sun . . . the lone homestead of the Hidden Valley . . . Erslinda lay in a fever. Erslinda, his little brown-eyed angel, whose tears could half break his heart and bring his rough brown face against her cheek. Erslinda, at eight years already the image of *la madrecita querida,* the dear little lost mother who had left them to be with her *Tata Dios.*

Eligio had left her, dying perhaps, with her two brothers. They were good brown mountain lads who knew what the sheep were saying when they cried out at night, and who did not mind talking to mountains alone in the moonlight, but who would run and hide when a stranger would appear in the *Valle.*

The two boys were with her. One, Toribio, would be down on his knees asking God to leave her with them; the other, Juanito, would be holding fast to her hand. Eligio battled down through the black woods to Vallecitos, with the whip of fear lashing him behind and one tiny hope to lead him: one little *cruz de Jesús* . . . one wooden crucifix on the altar in the church at the village, the cross that had cured Macrio Romero of the fever and saved José Adán that time of a doomed spring in the Valle Alamoso. If only Padre Onésimo would give him that crucifix. If only he could fight his way back to Erslinda before the red moon turned white over the tops of the firs and the coyotes came out talking their queer way on the hilltops!

There was a doctor in the village, too: old Pantureaux with his black bag and half-white whiskers. Eligio would see him for medicine, but, after all, what could one hope from a mere *médico* in such a case?

Three days ago, Toribio had come crying to the cabin, and sure enough when Eligio went out with him, there was old Chango, the biggest goat, on a stump inside the corral, standing upright like a man and preaching to the flock.

They could hear strange words beyond understanding and when Chango saw them coming there was a sudden red-fire circle around him. As it died away the old goat leaped down among the herd, saying "ba-a" in his own language again. A puff of heat came blowing past their ears that could only have been the breath of the very devil.

That night Juanito saw a great wolf go flying out of the trees the way a lost soul would fly. When the wolf appeared against the white moon, there was blue fire in his mouth and he dropped down suddenly and stood howling on a rock at the top of the hill.

When that night was halfway into dawn, two coyotes, slim wolf brothers of *el Demonio,* The Demon, sat on a hill and began a mad fandango to drive back the sun. Over across the valley one answered like a call from another world. Eligio knew the Voice, and it said, "Er-slinda, Er--rs--li-i-in-da!" over and over. As he lay in bed listening, he heard his little daughter moan softly in her sleep, but when he muttered a swift *Ave María* she was silent again; and outside the two coyotes went *yip-yirr-uping* back into the woods.

That morning Erslinda arose a little quieter, yet well and clear-eyed; but one mother goat was dead on her knees in the corral. When the boys had milked the others and Erslinda drank the milk, moon whiteness came over her face and the fever began to take her again. Juanito looked in her cup and sure enough, there, for a second, was the outline of a face marked in blue pinpoint bubbles of milk.

It was a devil's spring and a devil's fever that had come to the Valle Escondido. Eligio Jaramillo rode out of the black hills for the token of our Savior that would save his daughter . . . if not from death, at least from the *Diablo* who would take her soul away.

The river was a monster across his path. It swished down the cañon in a current so swift that every wave arched its back and leaped to keep up with its fellows like a wolf anxious to be in at the killing. Although the muddy rider knew it would be death, he urged the black horse to the river's edge. Black Choto groaned, but stepped into the torrent, for he knew his master. Two steps brought his head into the waves. The horse knew death when he saw it, and he saw it then, but it was not so close that a lunge and a desperate pawing of water did not bring him streaming and quaking back to the bank. Eligio's heart was a second without beating, for he knew poor Choto could not carry him across.

75

Yet he must cross. Twenty steps above, where the water came tearing out of the box cañon, it was narrower, and at the edge of the bank, the curled fingers of the flood clutched at the roots of a tall blue pine. If he had an ax he could chop it, and it might swish down and catch on the other bank, for the tree was long enough. But Eligio had left the Valle half in stupor from the dread in his soul and had not been foreminded. He tried pushing the tree. It swayed a little, for the water had loosened its roots, but it did not fall. A dozen little stones and a single block of black earth where he had disturbed the anchor of the tree tumbled into the stream, and no more.

The black horse stood like a slim statue back a bit from the bank, and Eligio looked at him without hope. Then suddenly he was at the saddle, unbuckling the lasso that always hung there. It was a long rope, light and tough the way the cowboys like; Eligio could throw it, too, with a swish that would fetch up whatever he caught in a quick surprise.

Now it was no running horse he must rope, but the snag roots of a big log lying like clusters of dead snakes across the Rito. He threw with all his might, and the slim string of the rope flew clear across the water. It did not catch, but it was long enough. It dropped down into the water and was dragged off down the stream, but Eligio pulled it to him swiftly and a spark of hope came into his heart. Now he could cross the river. It remained for him to throw the rope swiftly and surely.

And he did. The third time, the questing loop caught on a stout snag and held when the middle bellied to a strong tug of the raging water. He tied Black Choto to a bush back from the bank to await his return with *la cruz salvadora* before the moon would rise. Then he crept into the water, knotting his hands in the rope and fighting that giant a thousand times his strength with the muscles of a man and the heart of a *león*.

Eligio had come down out of the black woods where a *Lobo-Diablo,* a Devil Wolf, had flown across the moon, and he was going down to the Vallecitos for a Cross of Jesus to save the child that was his other heart, and he had crossed the river because. . . .

One step on the bank in safety and he heard the soft sound of a *woo-ooh* behind him. When he looked back, half in terror, it was the tall blue pine that was swaying down over the river. It came slowly to rest its stiff upper branches on a gray boulder across the river so that its trunk was a stout-bristled bridge over the water that any man might cross. If Eligio had only waited. . . .

But now he was over. With the coiled rope around his dripping shoulders he was on his way down the wild, curved road. Now he would run in the mud the few miles distance to the chapel, and he would be back across the pine-tree bridge before the moon! *Jesús adorado!*

Eligio ran like the cursing old river itself, for here there had been more sun on the road. But even as he went, dodging the black bog holes and talking a prayer to the good Jesus, there was a voice that muttered in the little cañons and a soft sound of doom in the wind; and the black hills talked behind him.

It was where the slanting road comes down by the river and a helpless old trail crawls to the west edge of the water, that his tired legs pulled him down to rest. And it was when he dropped his head in his leathered hands for a dead still moment that he heard the voice that called from over the river, the voice that called across the water.

"*Amigo! Amigo!*"

It was a strange sound. Eligio looked in wonder. Who would be calling from the old trail? Ah, what would the poor sheepman see? Leaning against the white trunk of a fallen tree, holding himself up with his arms out on two branches, as though he might be a Christ on the Cross, was a long-haired man with a curly brown beard on his face, and the black woods behind him. Eligio had not yet closed his mouth from surprise when the man stepped down to the brink of that rabid water and called again.

"*Amigo!* Friend! Help me to cross this water! I cannot pass it alone!"

Eligio saw that there was a stain of red, like blood, on his blue rag jacket and remembered how he had heard of the old hermit, digger of the mines, who was like to be standing on his head half of the day because of the crazy way he was.

So Eligio called to him that he could not cross that torrent, worse here than above. For it was only the crazy miner, and Eligio must be running on down the road to the village.

"Your rope! Throw me your rope!" the old man called out, now more insistently.

But Eligio was going again and would leave him there, for who would stop to help an old fool down? He looked back over his shoulder and his heart stopped for a second with his legs. The old man was wading in, arms over his head. He would be lost!

Let him drown! Eligio had battled to come down this far for the *cruz de Jesús,* and he must go on. But in his heart now he felt as if there were only one world and

78

one man in it, the crazy old man wading out to go down in the flood. And only Eligio could save him.

The hawk does not flick his wing more quickly than Eligio pulled the rope coils from his shoulder, ran back and whistled the strong maguey string across the water.

The line looped over the old man, and when he went strangling down under the flood, Eligio, caught the rope a turn around a stout white aspen and pulled him up again! It was one *hombrecito* against the whole weight of another and the long-muscled water besides, and there was death in it for one or both if Eligio should slip, for he had the rope wound about his hand and arm like a snake.

Eligio pulled and hauled and cursed like a crazy man and the old *minero* gurgled and fought the water and then went dead on the rope until a whirl caught and swung him past the middle. Eligio pulled him out on the bank like a great dead trout. But the old man was not dead.

There were two long, lost hours the sheepman was working with him until he stood up again, and now he would be too late getting back to Erslinda! He tried to run on now, but the *minero* plucked him by the sleeve and said, "Where do you go, my friend, and why do I see shadows like the black woods in your eyes?"

Ah, Eligio wanted to hurry away, but now he must stay and tell the old man what he asked, for there was no end to the look in his eyes. So he did tell him, even how Chango had preached to the flock up in the Valle and how he had come fighting across the river.

The *minero* gave him a look like the look of a clear blue sky and said: "Who shall say that the little roots are only for the growing of wild grass? Or that uphill is not down to the one who understands?"

Even before he had finished, Eligio was off again down the rough road to the village . . . late . . . late, but with half the fear shadow gone from his black eyes and he not knowing why.

At the beginning of evening Eligio came over the last hill with the gray sage clumps about him, to look upon the village down by the river where he would find the chapel and the Holy Crucifix.

The blackness rushed back into his heart when he looked, for the long digging arms of the water had crept out and clutched the old chapel, and the sun-baked mud of its walls was crumbling into the flood. As he ran crying down the hill the last front wall with the great cross upon it tumbled into the water and all the God-fearing people of the Vallecitos stood groaning and watching it. . . . All but the good Padre Onésimo, for his body was already somewhere down the river and his soul flying up to his *Tata Dios.*

Eligio Jaramillo had come down out of the black woods of talking wolves for the *cruz de Jesús* to save his daughter, but the black water was there before him. Even the good Padre who might have known the holy words to say for making another cross was gone.

Eligio took back a useless medicine from old Pantureaux; yet he was now without hope. How would a little red bottle of white pellets save the girl when there was blue fire in the mouth of a wolf flying across the moon? Now he must go back through the black woods to bury his dead, and his heart with her under the black earth. He had lost two hours fighting the river for a crazy digger of mines, and the avenging water had been that long before him at the chapel.

There was only one word in the woods as he climbed back again toward the Valle, and that was the shouting word of the river in the cañon. Eligio crossed the pine-tree bridge that had fallen for him. The water was singing a wild song beneath him. Now he would step down to die in it, but he must not, for the dead must be buried.

Black Choto was there by the foot of the hill with a strange, joyful voice welcoming his master, who had no ears for the sound of a poor horse's gladness.

It was slow up the mountain. The moon was white and going west over the black firs when Eligio topped the hill where the little coyotes should be out talking their queer way in the night. But there was no voice in the woods. Ah, the poor sheepman understood this silence of death in the Valle! For why should a devil-wolf be howling now that Eligio was coming back with empty hands . . . too late?

When he rode in the Valle with the black cabin up on the sunny ridge of it, there was a cry from the marsh by the road and when Eligio looked, it was the old *minero* again, deep in a bank of the melting snow of spring and calling:

"*Amigo!* Friend! Your rope! Throw me your rope!"

Eligio would kill him now, for his heart was black with grief. Yet he did not. Again it was in his heart that there was but one world and one man in it, and that was the old man dying there in the moonlit snow. He looped him again with the rope he threw that same sure way, and pulled him out flat where the snow was hard.

But he did not raise him up, for now he must ride on up the hill to kiss the dead lips of his Erslinda. *Ay! Jesús!*

It was the boy Toribio who ran out when Eligio

came to the cabin. But it was Erslinda, brown little sister of the angels, who stood in the light of the open door and called to him, her voice singing into his poor heart like the joy of a day that never was.

How could the man listen to his boy telling him something until Erslinda was in his arms and her face against his? For they must tell how a strange miner-man with a beard, and with the look of the blue sky in his eyes and red stains like blood on his jacket, had come wordlessly into the cabin, with queer grasses on his brow.

And when Erslinda drank the red drink the stranger brought for her from beneath his jacket, the fever left her, and they, falling on their knees at her bed, did not see him leave.

It was in a quiet moonlight that Eligio Jaramillo went quickly searching down the valley for the *minero* he had left lying on the snow. But the only thing to be found was the print where his clothes had stained the snow like a blood-red cross.

There is a holy calm that follows springtime where Eligio Jaramillo has built a red stone cross in the Valle Escondido in honor of the Holy Jesus, and the little coyotes talk their queer quiet way in the night.

THE HEXER

By Thomas Thompson

No one introduced me to John Brock, the man who came out to get the team the night we moved to the new farm Dad had bought out there at the edge of the swamp. But then, you really didn't need to be introduced.

It was the first time I had ever seen a hunchback, but that wasn't what you noticed first. He had eyebrows as thick as horses' tails, and when he chewed tobacco, which was always, those eyebrows bounced up and down and his coal black eyes sort of glittered through them, snapping on and off the way stars do through trees on a windy night. I knew right off he was as different as this new land we had come to, and the land sure was different from the Texas Panhandle we were used to.

My dad always had been fiddle-footed, and we were used to moving, because he'd work for first one cow outfit and then another, but this time he really pulled up stakes.

He had been working for Mr. Charles Goodnight there in the Palo Duro, and he had just come back from trail driving a herd up to Dodge. I knew the minute I looked at him he had something big on his mind because he was grinning from ear to ear, but I don't guess any of us were ready for it when he said, "It's California, Mother. That's where we're headed!"

Far into that night Dad and Mother sat there in the kitchen, the lamp throwing a big circle of light on the maps and railroad folders Dad had brought back from Dodge. The big California gold rush was long past, but according to those railroad folders, the real gold was still there in the ground. All you had to do to get it was plow, put in seeds, and sit back and watch 'em grow. In a place called the San Joaquin Valley, wheat and barley grew as high as a man on horseback, and there was always work for a good cowhand—which my dad was—because there were cattle on a thousand hills. My mother hinted we could just go up to Kansas and get some railroad land, but Dad said, "And face grasshoppers and blizzards and cattlemen tearing down your fences? No siree, Bob! It's California for us."

And that's the way it was. The land he took was in the swamp country along the Kaweah River in the San Joaquin Valley of California. As for John Brock, well, he just seemed to come along with the place.

John Brock was a Missouri man. He had fought in the War Between the States and been mixed up in the Kansas-Missouri Border troubles. Some said he had gotten run out of there and couldn't go back. I don't know. All I knew for sure then was he was here in California, the same as us. Folks called him a swamp rat and he did odd jobs and that's about all we knew. But we were going to find out a whole lot more than that.

He was a man who could do almost anything. He could witch wells and make medicine out of green grapefruit and manzanita leaves and he was always digging up strange roots and drying different kinds of bark and nobody knew just what he did with those things. I was afraid to ask.

John was the only one who had ever really seen the ghost mare that lived out there in the swamp. Dad said it was just an old stray mare, but my brother Hamp and I weren't so sure. John told how he had seen her that night, fire squirting out of her nostrils, her chains rattling in the dark. . . . Dad said the Sutton boys had caught this old stray and tied a chain to her tail and turned her loose just as John was coming through the swamp one night. Some people believed that, but some didn't, and I was one of those who didn't. There was a ghost mare out there, all right. There were lots of strange things in the swamp you couldn't see, but you knew they were there.

It was a wonderful place to live. Mom and Dad had a tent-house with a wooden floor, and Hamp and I had a tent of our own, right under a big weeping willow tree. Cliff Price, who was a cousin of Dad's and just a little older than my brother, came to live with us, and bit by bit we got the ground cleared and the stumps pulled and the farm started taking shape.

The days were busy, with us burning brush and cutting bean poles, and finally the ground was ready to plant potatoes. Those were the good times, because John Brock came to help us, and that's when I started hearing all the stories he told. About how it had rained frogs in Missouri, and about the hoop snake that put its tail in its mouth and rolled along. It had a stinger so poisonous, it would kill a tree right in front of your eyes. One time John had tried to straddle one with a team, and the hoop snake got its stinger caught in the wagon tongue. That wagon tongue swelled up and pushed the team right off the road.

There were other stories, too, as we sat there in the main tent house, cutting potatoes to the eye and getting the gunny sacks cut just right so they'd fit over your shoulder and you could drop the cut potatoes "eye side up" into the furrow.

We were just about ready to plant, but John Brock went out and looked at the moon and when he came back inside he shook his head. "Can't plant tomorrow," he said. "Moon ain't right. 'Taters will rot sure." We did what he said, because there was no doubt about it, John had a lot of magic powers. Cliff Price was the only one who didn't believe in him. Cliff laughed at everything John said, and that's what finally got him in big trouble.

It happened right after I got into a little bit of trouble myself. Dad sent me out to plant cantaloupes. It was a hot day and I'd walk along, dig with the hoe, drop in eight seeds, cover the hole and tamp it, take eight long steps and do it all over again. After about three rows, I got tired. I don't know what ever made me do it, but I just dug one deep hole and put all the seeds I had left into it and covered it up. As soon as I had done it I wished I hadn't, because I knew those seeds would all come up in one spot and then Dad would know what I had done and I'd be in real trouble . . . Well, that's when I went to John Brock, because I just didn't know where else to go.

What I had in mind was for John to hex those seeds

so they wouldn't grow. Oh, he could hex, all right, but he didn't much like to talk about it. The way he explained it, the more you talk about hexing, the more your hexing loses its power. I remember how he sat there, chewing away on his Cotton Boll Twist, his eyebrows bouncing and his eyes glittering and finally he said, "I could hex the seeds, but it still wouldn't get rid of what you done wrong, would it?" I had to admit that was right, but I sure wanted out of this mess bad, so he finally said all right, that night we'd take care of it.

It was spooky out there in the cantaloupe patch, what with the frogs chunking and the mosquitoes buzzing and every time one bit me I got to worrying I'd get malaria sure and have to take calomel and then maybe even salivate . . . John had told me all about salivating, and it was awful. If you took calomel and then ate anything sour or sweet your teeth would fall out and your bones would get all soft. What you had to do was take Epsom salts to get rid of the calomel, and I guess there isn't anything tastes worse. What with the ghost mare out there roaming around, and me worried about salivating and John digging away in the ground just like he was digging a grave . . . well, I don't want to go through that night again.

Finally John had three buckets full of dirt. He packed two and I packed one and we went back to the tent where we could have some light. Of course we had to tell Cliff and Hamp what I had done, but they promised they wouldn't tell.

John made a sifter out of an old window screen and we set up most of the night, sifting out those seeds. I was so tired I would have gone to sleep, but I couldn't, because that was the night John told us the most about hexing. Hamp and I sat there bug-eyed and Cliff kept laughing and John's voice kept droning on and on. Once when I went outside, you could see their shadows climbing up the wall of the tent. The tule fog was swirling around my ankles, and the sour smell of fresh-cut cottonwood was in the air, mingling with the fragrance of the damp salt grass and the alkali. The swamp sounds were everywhere . . . It wasn't hard to believe John could hex people.

Hamp and Cliff helped me get the cantaloupe seeds planted, and all the while we kept talking about hexing. Then all of a sudden Cliff said, "Let's try it." Hamp said he didn't know if we should or not, but Cliff said he would prove there was nothing to it. We could hex him.

I sure didn't want any part of it, but they were older than I was and after all, they had promised to keep still about me burying all the seeds in one spot. They made me cross my heart and hope to die, and I went into the swamp with them.

Usually the swamp isn't too scary in daylight, but that day it was. The wild grapevines we always swung on were hanging down like jungle snakes across our path. The deeper we got into the swamp, the more gnarled and twisted the trees became. Every sound was sharp and clear, like a pistol shot, and I kept thinking about the ghost mare, and at every step I expected old Fuqua to step out in front of us. Fuqua was supposed to have a tail like a monkey, although nobody had ever really seen it. He lived out here alone, and even the grown-ups were afraid of him because he always carried a shotgun loaded with rock salt, and he would just as soon give you both barrels as look at you.

Hamp gave Cliff a chance to back out, but Cliff just laughed. He sure did want to show John Brock up, he said, and he swore he was with the Sutton boys the night they tied the chain to the old mare's tail. That Cliff just didn't believe in anything. He even went so far as to pick out the tree himself.

It was a big, slick-bark alder, growing out of a little hummock of ground. It was tall and straight with the bottom limbs coming out about six feet off the ground. Alders have a damp smell all their own and the air was full of it, and that smooth bark was just inviting someone to carve his name. Hamp said, "You sure?" And Cliff said, "If you don't start carving, I'll do it myself. I'm sick and tired of listening to John Brock's wild tales." My brother took out his pocket knife.

Now that we had actually started it, hexing seemed almost too simple to be true. What you do is carve a picture of the one you want hexed on the bark of a tree. It doesn't really have to look like him, just so you name who it is, and that picture Hamp carved sure didn't look a lot like Cliff. The main thing is, you name it, and then you take a tenpenny nail and you put it right between the picture's eyes. Every day you go out to the tree and say *"Shuli, shuli, shuli poppa que. Shuli pop a zig zag, tillie come a roo."* You bear down real hard on the *ROO,* and when you do, you hit that nail—just once. When the nail is all the way in, the one you're hexing is dead.

The more Hamp carved, the less funny it seemed, and I guess Hamp felt that way too, because he wanted to stop, but Cliff wouldn't hear of it. Finally he got mad and took the knife away from Hamp and finished the picture himself, but he made Hamp start the nail and say the magic words because, of course, you can't hex yourself. Cliff was laughing so hard he was doubled over. "I sure want to see that old windbag's face when I bring him out here and show him this," he said. He was still laughing when he headed back home, but my brother was very quiet and I felt like a dozen spiders were crawling up my backbone.

Hamp and Cliff said they'd kill me if I told John what we were up to and I guess they would have, so I didn't tell. A couple of times I went with them and a couple of times I didn't, but every day they went back to that big slick-bark alder in the middle of the swamp, said the magic words of *"Shuli, shuli, shuli poppa que"* and hit that nail another whomp with the big rock. And on the fifth day, Cliff started to get sick.

I looked at my brother and he looked at me, and we both knew what the other one was thinking. We had to get out there quick, pull that nail, and stop the hex.

I never put in such a day in my life. We had Cliff's chores to do as well as our own, and it was one of those days when Dad found a million extra things for us to do. When we went in to supper, there was Cliff, his face all red, not talking, and we couldn't talk to him because Mom and Dad were right there. Mom had made some soup, but Cliff couldn't even swallow that, he was that sick. It was almost dark when we finally got away.

We ran all the way out to the big alder and when we got there we were both so out of breath our bellies hurt. My brother's hands were shaking so bad he could hardly hold the rock. That old alder suddenly looked like its limbs were reaching down for us and it kept getting darker and the ground fog started seeping up the legs of our overalls. Hamp started working on that nail, pounding it first one way and then the other, trying to loosen it, but the green wood had swelled up around it, and it wouldn't move. It seemed to me that all he was doing was driving it in deeper. He gave it another try, but the nail bent over, flat against the bark of the tree. It was then I was sure I heard chains rattling, and I started to run. When I looked back, Hamp was right behind me.

When we got to the main tent-house we were all out of breath, and Mom said, "What have you two been doing?" and Hamp said, "Playing." She told us we shouldn't play so hard, but we hardly heard her because we wanted to see Cliff. When we looked at him, I was sorry we had. He was burning up with fever, and his eyes were all glazed and funny looking and he just kept staring at us as if he had never seen us before.

We got out of there quick, and we sure didn't have an easy time of it going to sleep. I dozed off, and about midnight Hamp shook me and woke me up. He had a lantern and claw hammer. "Get your clothes on," he said. "We're going back out there."

"I'm scared," I said.

"So am I," he said, "but you're going anyway."

That was a night I won't forget. We didn't light the lantern for fear somebody would see us. The tule fog was wispy and reaching out at us with long, wet fingers, and every piece of brush grabbed at us as we went by. We lost the trail and finally Hamp had to light the lantern and then it was worse than ever, because the shadows of our legs reached out into the darkness as if they were searching for trouble, and I knew they were. When we got to the alder it was even worse.

Hamp had me hold the lantern up so he could see. It

threw a light on Cliff's picture that made it look more like a skull than a face. The sap had started to run and it trickled down the face like black blood. The frogs were making an awful racket. Hamp started working on the nail, but his hands were shaking so badly he wasn't getting much of anywhere, and then all of a sudden the frogs stopped and it was dead quiet, and in that quiet we heard footsteps.

I dropped the lantern and grabbed onto Hamp and he grabbed onto the tree and then the voice, low and growling, said, "What are you kids doing out here?" I knew it was Fuqua and I expected to hear the blast of his shotgun and feel the sting of rock salt, and then John Brock stepped out into the circle of lantern light.

I don't think I ever heard my brother talk that fast before and I never will again. He told John everything.

For a long time John just stood there, holding the lantern up to Cliff's picture, chewing away, his eyes glittering through his eyebrows, and then he said, "You boys got a peck of trouble here, but maybe I can straighten it out." He stuck his face right close to mine. "You two keep your mouths shut about this, you hear?" He sure didn't have to tell us twice.

He picked up the hammer and walked over to the tree and took a long, hard look at Cliff with the sap-blood running down his face and without looking at us he said, "Doctor was out to see Cliff tonight."

That was about the best news I had ever heard and my words came out with a big whoosh of breath. "What'd he say?"

John turned on me as if I had slapped him in the face. "What do you expect he said? Doctors don't know nothin'.

Even if they did, you figger one could fix a hex like this? Now you two skedaddle on home before you're missed. Me, I got a lot of consortin' with ha'nts and witches to do. Might even have to get a couple of hairs from the ghost mare's tail. And don't you say a word to nobody or you're gonna undo everything I'm fixin' to do."

We got out of there, fast. I felt as if somebody was breathing right down my neck, and I kept walking faster and faster and finally I was in a full run. That tent sure did look good. I jumped under the covers with all my clothes on and Hamp did the same.

When we went in to breakfast the next morning, there was old Cliff sitting up, trying to eat some fried eggs, but he was having a hard time of it. His face was all swollen up and he was real wobbly, but there wasn't any doubt he was better. My dad came in and took a look at him and said, "Boy, you got about as fine a case of mumps as I ever seen. Both sides."

The first minute we could, Hamp and I got John Brock aside. "Dad says Cliff has mumps," I said.

John just glowered at me. "Course he has," he said. "I tried to change that hex into measles, but when you bent that nail you sort of gouged it into his jowls."

And there wasn't any doubt about that. Cliff's jowls sure were swollen up.

John had stayed up all night breaking the hex, he said. He showed us a couple of white hairs from the tail of the ghost mare. We put them in the horse trough where John said in time they'd turn into snakes and sure enough they did.

That night he came out to the tent with a jar full of that green grapefruit-manzanita leaf brew of his, boiled down until it was as thick as syrup. It was as bitter as gall, but Hamp and I gulped it down without a word. Even then, he said, he wasn't sure he could keep us from getting the mumps—because of the part we'd had in the hex. And as it worked out, he was right. Hamp and I both got the mumps, but only on one side, so that wasn't so bad.

Cliff never did laugh at John Brock again, and he even admitted he'd been lying about being with the Sutton boys when they tied the chain to the tail of that stray mare.

So I guess the old ghost mare is still out there. I don't know. The swamp has a lot of secrets it never gives up, but I think the best kept secret is still the one about the time we almost hexed poor old Cliff.

.

JOHNNY WHO RODE THE GHOST TRAIN

By Phoebe and Todhunter Ballard

A mirage, of course, as defined by the dictionary, is an optical phenomenon produced by a stratum of hot air of varying density across which the observer sees reflections of some distant object.

In southern Arizona, between the Little Dragoon Mountains on the north—a brown, bare spine of rock lying like the skeleton of a dinosaur—and the rugged peaks of the Dragoons proper on the south, where Cochise made his stronghold—there stretches a dry lake, barren of growth, white, flat, forbidding, and dead. Nothing lives there, nothing moves there. Yet periodically a train, smoke boiling from its bell stack, was seen to cross the bleak expanse. Those who had seen it claimed they could hear the busy chuff of the engine and the clatter of wheel flanges on iron rails. The train appeared to be crossing a glittering blue lake, as if the blowing sand recalled an ancient memory of the time when that vast emptiness was a living sea bed.

But the nearest right-of-way ran on the far side of the distant mountains.

No one in his right mind ever thought to ride this ghost train. Certainly not Johnny Cowden.

Johnny was a young man with a single purpose: prospecting. He had a quick wit, a solid intelligence, and a ready grin. Together they made him a favorite at the scattered ranch houses, the isolated mines and the boom towns of the Southwest.

But for all his gregariousness, Johnny was a loner at his trade, and despite his youth he had already covered most of the Arizona and New Mexico mining districts. He was driven by restlessness, and the fact that he had not yet made a strike to net him more than a few hundred dollars. He was a true prospector and he had utter faith that just over the next rocky ridge lay his El Dorado.

So, when in the late eighteen-seventies he heard the whisper on the wind of a new silver excitement in the Dos Cabezas mountains, he left Tombstone and headed northeast.

He was in a hurry. All prospectors are when they hear the siren call of a fresh strike—certain that unless they reach the ground at once all of the valuable claims will have been staked. Johnny took his bearings with his mind's eye on the shortest route, and outfitted himself to meet his demands.

It was midsummer. The temperature hovered around a hundred and ten and up and he figured he had some seventy miles to cross between water holes. But he was strong and filled with confidence. He had a burro, lightly loaded, with a minimum of his possessions. And besides his canteen he had a water bag of his own invention. It was made of heavy canvas sides that allowed just enough evaporation to cool the water slightly. He had devised it after studying the Mexican pottery *ollas* hanging in the shade of the roofed sidewalks throughout the border towns.

He calculated that starting fresh he could cut across the Dragoons in one day, camp and rest on the shore of the dry lake, and when night came push on directly across it. The lake was the waterless stretch, and too hot to cover in the daytime.

He could have detoured around it and headed north to pick up the Wilcox stage road. But he would save a whole day by going straight across the level bed, and it was easier walking as long as he didn't get lost. Out in the middle there was no horizon except the stretching white sand, but at night he could steer his course by the stars.

Johnny made good time, occasionally glancing at Lime Peak off his left shoulder and trying to ignore the sun, his wide hat pulled down against its burning rays. He reached the last slope of foothills above the lake and camped in the shade of a rock burst. If he slept until sundown he would be able to cross the lake bed and reach the stage road on the north shore sometime in the next afternoon. Then he would rest again, and the last leg into the new camp would be a cinch.

He watered the burro, had his sparing drink and shared his cold biscuits with the little animal. He did not picket it. In hundreds of miles of travel with him, the jenny had never strayed more than a few yards from camp. He did pull off the pack saddle with its provisions and precious bag of water so that the burro too could rest. He beat the brush for snakes, dug his hip holes and wriggling into a comfortable position, he went to sleep.

He was wakened by a scream. He lay for an instant,

orienting himself and the sound, then grabbed the rifle from the ground at his side and came to his feet. He recognized the scream of a hunting cat and he knew it was the burro that the beast would be after.

It was dark and he had overslept. That was his second reaction—that he should have been on his way long before now. His first concern was the jenny. He could not see much and he went forward cautiously, listening for further sounds.

What he heard warned him that the cat had already made its kill, and his hands tightened on the gun. But he never got to shoot. By the time he found the slaughtered burro, the cat had torn what it wanted from the small body and vanished into the rocky hills.

Johnny stood beside the mangled carcass and a hard lump rose in his throat. He and the burro had covered many strikes together, many lonely miles, and the little beast had never failed him. But sentiment was not enough to turn him aside, to make him follow the killer's trail to take revenge. He had a call that he must answer.

He turned back to camp, his eyes accustomed to the dark now, and stopped, staring in consternation. In its blind flight from the attacking cat, the burro had blundered through the mound of supplies beside the empty pack saddle, scattering them beyond recovery. But it wasn't the burst flour sack or the end of bacon ground into the gritty soil that made Johnny groan. It was the water sack, lying flat and empty against the rocks, ripped open by the burro's sharp hoof.

Johnny had never needed profanity and he wasted no time in cursing now. He picked up the side of bacon and half a dozen dried biscuits, wiped them on his sleeve, then tested the canteen. It was better than half full. Holding it, he looked off across the dry lake, weighing his chances.

The moon was up. A silver sheet covered the enormous flatness, so wide that Johnny fancied he could see the curvature of the earth. The sensible thing would be to head back south, re-outfit and try again. But prospectors are gamblers. The lake lay cool and inviting, and without the lagging burro he should be able to walk six or seven miles an hour. Johnny hesitated only a moment. Then he took a small drink from the canteen by way of a toast to his fortune, and started out.

The walk through the night was easy. The moon gave him his direction, and the sand was hard packed under his boots. Yet when daylight came the world was still as flat as an ocean around him. He could not see the low ridge of rocks that would tell him he was nearing the far shore. He could only go forward and hope to make it across before the sun would strike him down.

It looked like a ball of fire rising out of the haze in the eastern sky, and as it rose the heat increased until the air waves rising from the sand tasted like the breath of a blast furnace. When it was overhead Johnny knew that in all his years on the frontier he had never known such heat. His senses grew sluggish and the hot haze that rose around him was like a curtain, hard to see through. He felt his body tissues crawl as the moisture was sucked from him. His tongue was growing too large for his mouth. If only there were shade, just a little shade to relieve for a few moments the monotonous beat of the sun—but there was none. The floor of the lake remained bare, as though it had been scraped by a blade.

He stopped, anchoring his feet against their tendency

to stumble, and sipped from the canteen. He had taken many sips in the last five hours and the bottle was distressingly light. The sip only aggravated his thirst. He felt that he could drink a sea of water, that his body was drying like jerked meat.

He lurched on. At about four o'clock he swallowed the last of the water, almost boiling now, and heaved the useless canteen away. Peculiarly, the unburdening of the light vessel seemed to give him added strength. He straightened, and for a quarter of a mile pushed forward at increased speed. If he could only last until sunset!

Suddenly he became aware of a second set of tracks. He stared at them, his dulled mind trying to focus on the unbelievable possibility that there was another human being out on this vast emptiness, another man who might have water. Then very slowly his brain cleared into suspicion. He lifted a foot and placed it in the boot print ahead of him. The tracks were his own. He had been traveling in a circle, and he did not know for how long. In his daze he must have forgotten to check the position of the blazing globe above.

Johnny sat down and cried from exhaustion and frustration, although there was no moisture left in him for tears. He continued to sit, not because he had given up, but because he had no idea where he was or which way to start again.

Why walk when each step would probably take him deeper again into the waste? Better to wait for darkness, if he could endure that long. Then the moon would at least give him the points of the compass.

So he sat in the merciless glare trying to hold on to his wavering senses. Then he saw the mirage.

At first it was only water—perhaps a wishful hallucination—blue water and waves flooding across the dead lake. Johnny struggled up, reaching forward instinctively, then dropping his hand, for he still had wits enough to recognize it for what it was. The image grew sharper, terrifyingly real. Johnny squeezed his eyes closed, and when he opened them he saw the train.

It was coming toward him at an angle. Every detail of the big chuffing engine and the two yellow painted cars behind were as sharply distinct as a lithograph. Smoke rolled from the fat stack and blew back across the water. Johnny had heard stories about this train ever since he had come into the country, but he had never seen it before. It moved steadily, deliberately through the waves without disturbing them, and he could see no rails. He watched it, fear sharpening his fading senses, making him forget his thirst.

Then a rage broke in him. It was bad enough that he was doomed to die here, but why must this vision appear to mock him? If this were a real train, if this water were real, he would be saved.

He heard a whistle, the clang of a bell and the whine of wheels on an uneven track. Hysteria washed away his rage. Johnny began to laugh, to jump up and down, to wave his arms. Then he heard himself screaming—he knew his mind had broken—screaming at the top of his lungs, yet no sound came from his parched throat. The only sound was the steady throbbing of the coming train.

He watched in fascinated horror as it headed directly for the spot where he stood, looming larger and larger, the brass rim of the headlight glinting. The two big drivers locked by their bar spun monstrously and the sooted face of the engineer craned from the cab.

Johnny's every fiber cried to him to run, to dive for safety before the heavy flanges crushed out what life remained in him, but where he had stomped and whooped a moment before, now he stood paralyzed, unable to move. At the last moment the vision was refracted away. It would not grind over him. It would pass him within four or five feet.

It did not pass. The roaring engine came abreast of Johnny, the brake shoes screamed as they bit against the wheel rims, the couplings crashed together and the train stopped. Like some puffing monster it stood, steam hissing from the engine and from the connectors between the cars. Johnny could almost have reached out and touched it, but he did not dare.

Then the door at the end of the second car opened. A blue-coated conductor swung down the high steps and stood beside them, calling:

"Board! All aboard!"

Johnny heard it clearly but he could not move, and the voice rose in impatience.

"Come on, come on, we're behind time already." The conductor pulled a turnip watch and read it. "Fifteen minutes late now, and we weren't supposed to make this stop."

He looked toward the engine and raised his hand in the hi-ball sign. The whistle shrilled, the drivers began to turn, protesting. The conductor stalked forward, caught Johnny's arm and wrenched him from the place where he was rooted, boosting him up the steps to the car platform as the car jerked into motion.

Johnny stumbled against the heavy door, without the

strength to open it. The conductor reached across him, swung it inward and, supporting Johnny, shoved him through.

The car was well filled. There was the white blur of curious faces, the acrid smells of coal smoke and tobacco, then Johnny's vision reeled as the conductor steered him, pushed him down into a seat.

Johnny did not think that he lost consciousness. He heard the murmur of sympathetic voices above him through a blacked-out haze. He heard one man say:

"Poor guy, he's had a real rough time. He's about done in."

"Water." It was an unintelligible word that came from Johnny's throat. "Water. Water."

"Hey, he's coming around." There was astonishment in the tone. "Get a cup of water, but don't give him too much."

Johnny opened his eyes, expecting to see the conductor, the passengers of the car. Instead he saw strangers, a room, a window with words painted on it. Johnny closed and opened his eyes again, not knowing what to believe, what was real and what was fantasy. But the water felt real as it crossed his cracked lips and swollen tongue. His body accepted it as real.

They gave him only a little at first although he begged for more. They gave it to him in drops, allowing time for it to seep through his tissues, and finally, when he could frame the words, he asked where he was.

They told him he was in the sheriff's office in Wilcox, that a man named Markham had found him stumbling around in circles about five miles outside town. They knew who he was. They asked where he had come from.

He told them, told about the burro and crossing the lake, told them about the train. They nodded in understanding. Thirst and the desert heat make for strange imaginings.

He asked what day it was, and when they told him, Johnny set his chin stubbornly. Markham had found him just after sundown of the day he had spent on the lake bed. It was impossible for him to have walked to Wilcox between four o'clock and sundown, in the best of condition. There were too many miles between.

He said so, and repeated the story of the train picking him up.

They told him he had his dates mixed. Johnny insisted. He knew when he had left Tombstone, knew when he had entered the dry lake. They told him the sun had done its work on him, had addled his brain.

But Johnny Cowden knew what he knew and no argument would ever convince him he was wrong. He had seen the train, he had heard it, he had ridden it. He stuck to his story, and before he left the Wilcox sheriff's office he had earned the nickname "Crazy Johnny" that followed him forever after.

GHOST WOLF OF THUNDER MOUNTAIN

By Will Henry

I had the story from the lips of the man it concerned most. Therefore I am confident in relating it.

This was in the Sangres country, when New Mexico was many legends younger than it is now. If I said the exact place was the ranch of Don Gaspar de Portogo on the Agua Piedra, certain *ancianos* would understand precisely what family and what rancho were intended. Yet, of course, the actual names would still be protected from today's pack of rascals and trespassers, that collective amoeba of man's curiosity which will seep in any place where the Pale One has been before them. So, call the rancho, Agua Piedra, and its master, Don Gaspar. And call the great mountain which towers beyond the river and the grassy slopes and the juniper flats, *El Trueno,* because that is not its true name, either, but very close to it. Ah, Old Ones, do I see you nod and smile? Certainly. You know the peak I mean.

The season was early winter. Upon my arrival, the Christmas festivities had barely begun, but at week's end they had reached the carnival stage that we, the transplanted children of Coronado and Cabeza de Vaca regard as just the proper excitement for the Feast of the Christ Child.

Do not believe that the guest list was composed of far travelers and affluent, such as myself. Nothing like that. Don Gaspar was the *patrón* of an area larger than some states of the first American colonies. The good flock gathered at his elegant hacienda was composed principally of those he called "his children." They in turn, with vast respect, addressed him as *el patrón*. These were the *vaqueros* who guarded his cattle, the *pastores* and *zagalos* who tended his sheep, the storekeepers, blacksmiths, cooks, and people of all degree who, with their broods of brown-eyed, beautiful little ones and, of course, their buxom, white-toothed women, were the "family" of Don Gaspar and of the Agua Piedra.

But this is not their story, except in a related way—as brothers are related, yet different.

On the night of which I tell, the merrymaking had achieved that riotous pitch the Americans mistakenly call a fandango—a wild dance without morals, leading but to mayhem and to marital as well as martial strife. Well, it was true some were dancing. And many, many, were shouting on the dancers and also the guitar and marimba players who lured the dancers to their gay gyrations. Added to this *baile* were the shrieks and laughter of children jousting to break the hanging clay baskets of bright gifts which decorated the rafters of the *sala grande,* and the clapping yelps of encouragement from the older ones who had passed the time of dancing in their lives. Well, a fact must be granted—something very like a fandango was going forward. But, then, these children of my own blood were not mingled with any but their own kind that evening. Only smiles flashed, and no knives.

Entering the *sala,* I searched at once for some less tumultuous haven. Presently, I spied it; the far side of the room where the giant fireplace gave light and warmth to the eyes and bones of the oldsters clustered there. Their backs were hunched to the gaiety behind them, and they relived their own *bailes,* far greater than this one. They complained that in other days the children behaved themselves in a much more decorous fashion, while the young men were far more mannerly. And the young women, *por Dios,* would not dream of showing anything like as much ankle, calf, and, God bear it witness! even *knee!*

Knowing this coterie from yesterday as the most compatible for a man of my own persuasions and, yes, admit it, of better Christmases gone by, I made my way around the crowded wall. I had reached the hearth and found my seat beside a grandly handsome octogenarian *vaquero*—or had he been, indeed, *caballero?*—and was loading my pipe when it happened.

I had never heard such a sound before, nor have I since.

It was a long, quavering cadence of sorrow, indescribably mournful, and yet its burden came not into that room as sadness but as naked fear. Down it came, through the silvered, hoarfrost air of the December night, falling from the bleak granite ramparts of *El Trueno,* Thunder Mountain, to spread like some chill from the other world among the gay dancers in Don Gaspar's hacienda. The pause was but that of an instant. There was a nervous shuffling of feet and coughing of throats and, here and there, false, tittering laughter. Some young men, in bravado, spoke aloud. One child began sobbing. The older people were universally silent. It was a very disturbing moment. It passed only because Don Gaspar alertly ordered the musicians to resume at once. This they did, with an irresistible rendition of "Jalisco!"

But the spell was not broken so swiftly that I had not time to note the peculiar action of the most grizzled of the graybeards by the fire. The old fellow had started up eagerly, as the great wolf's sobbing cry had echoed down the mountain. He had remained in a tense attitude of listening, long after the final eerie note had quivered away in the distance, and long after it had been lost in the now returned rhythms of the marimba players.

You have guessed already that the old fellow was the one I had first been attracted to: he of the noble face and white locks to the shoulder, he beside whom I had made my seat. Presently I addressed him softly.

"The wolf calls to you, *señor;* what does he say?"

He looked sharply at me. He was certainly startled, but I also detected what might have been gratitude in the old eyes.

"You do not jest, *señor?* You do not ridicule me?"

"But of course not, Old One. I sympathize. I am in accord. I would hear what you may have to tell me."

He nodded and returned to what I thought was his endless gazing into the embers of the fire. But I had not lost him, nor he his memories.

"I was once young," he began, "even as they who

click the heel and stamp the boot, there where the music sounds. Rich I was in land and sheep and cattle. For wife I had one of great beauty and God-given graces. The good Christ had seen fit, as well, to bless us with a beautiful son. To this *hijo* belonged our total lives. He was the light which lit the pathways of our existence. Do you understand?"

"But of course," I bowed. "Please continue."

"Almost daily was this son in my company, from the first birthday onward. Always was he guarded with extreme caution lest harm befall him. You see, it had befallen that, in his birth, some damage was done. My wife could bear no other child. Thus in the boy we dwelled to a degree not healthy. Eventually, such bondage as we forced upon the poor little lad became unbearable to him. He longed, just once, to wander forth without the guard of *vaqueros* which followed me, as I followed him.

"'Please, *padre*,' he would beg of me. '*Por favor*, only this one time allow me to see the land by myself. There is something out there which seems to call to me, and I want to go and find out what it is.'"

The old man paused, shaking his silvered head.

"You will recognize this was strange talk coming from a little boy of but a few summers' age. But I was not old and wise, then, and I answered the lad impetuously and without good reason told him no.

"The springtime softened into the summer and those brief golden days of August came and went—like heat lightning, and like our youth, splendid and exciting, yet also strangely muffled and, oh! so very swift and soon gone—and after that came the autumn and the red leaves and the yellow on the slopes and in the river bottoms.

Soon the first fall of snow lay on the shoulders of *El Trueno,* mantling his palisades to the first flats and benches above the valleys.

"One day toward the fall of evening my little son was not to be found. It was full starlight when we discovered upon one of the higher flats, amid the juniper and greasewood, his small tracks, dim and lonely, leading off through the thin snowfall up the north slope of *El Trueno.* As my *vaqueros* set off urgently pursuing this faint trail, slowed of course by the darkness and by the treacherous footing for their horses, the penetrating scream of the panther was heard from above us and in the direction those tiny footprints led. And more. Even as my men and I exchanged fearful glances at this first dread sound, it was overlain by a second cry, far more compelling than that of the panther. It was *el grito del lobo,* the marrow-freezing hunger cry of the great gray timber wolf.

"Esteban Chavez, my *mayordomo,* looked at me.

" '*El lobo llama,*' he said, 'I am afraid; I think he calls to us.'

" 'Lead on, Esteban,' I replied.

"He gave me a sorrowing glance. The men did the same. But they put spurs to mounts and went on up the icy slope because they loved me and my small son.

"We came to a very dangerous switchback in the trail, then a topping-out place, studded with boulders and scrub-like pines. There before our eyes lay the signs of disaster. The broad paw of the panther showed in the snow, joining the track of my son.

"Chavez knew this particular panther. It had had the two central toes of the left forefoot cut off by one of our traps. Chavez and the men called this great cat, *La*

Sombra, the Shadow. The story told around the *campos* of our sheep and cattle herdsmen was that this animal was a female bigger than any male, and more—that she was not of the pure mountain lion blood, such as the panthers we knew and called pumas. Rather, she had for a sire some wandering Mexican jaguar male, up here in the Sangres, God knows how, on a wanderlust of hunger.

"This *La Sombra,* then, was not as other pumas, which will not harm man, not even his children or his woman. She was a killer of men and had murdered three of my own *pastores,* two of them only young boys."

Again the old man paused, his memory reaching back along the dim track of time.

"I became as one possessed," he resumed. "I threw all caution to the freezing winds and raced along the difficult trail. Suddenly, the final spark of my hope was plunged out. There, before my eyes, a third track joined the previous two. I stared down in disbelief at the great, splay-footed mark of *El Lobo.*

"We called him only that, *El Lobo—the* Wolf. And we said it that way, marking a line under the *the* with our tongue. All knew which wolf was meant: *El Lobo,* the most dreaded animal in New Mexico. Some said, even, that he had been feared when Oñate and Díaz and Pedro Alvarado rode here, calling all this land New Spain. Some still say this. You saw their faces but a breath ago, when the great cry sobbed down from the mountain, eh?"

"*Si, anciano,*" I nodded. "I saw them. Pray continue."

"As you will, *señor.* I stood but a moment hypnotized by the mark of the huge foot in the snow. Then I raced on as before, caring not for *La Sombra* or *El Lobo* or for God or Christ or the Holy Ghost, even, but only for my son. I was in my own mind become greater than my Savior. Here was no place for the Prince of Peace. This was a time for the Avenger, and I was that one. My rifle was ready, my knife and my pistol, too. With my bare hands I would have attacked either beast, or both. Hope was dead but revenge was mine.

"In my madness I forged far ahead of my followers, in this manner coming first upon the tragedy.

"The way that the panther's tracks read in the snow, I knew that I stood behind the very boulder from which the bestial cat had hurled herself upon my son. I lunged beyond the fatal rock, dreading to have my worst fears confirmed, yet insane with vengeance.

"*Señor,* you will be hard-pressed to accept it. Rounding that great stone, I fell headlong over a huddled mass, measuring my length on the trail beyond. Sitting up, I beheld the monster carcass of *La Sombra,* rigid in that death which for her was but an experience she had meted out to countless pitiful others. Her enormous, whiskered head was thrown aside and lay at a grotesque angle. The white throat ruff was dyed crimson, the throat itself ripped open ear-base to ear-base."

"*El Lobo?*" I interjected quietly.

"The same, *señor.* In the one fearsome strike, he had smashed her down as lightning rives the mighty pine. But why, *señor?* That is what had Esteban Chavez and my men staring about into the black night and muttering as they crossed themselves.

"We searched the mountainside for any sign of my son. Nothing was discovered until, hidden in the sheltered bottom of a small *cañada*—you know, *señor,* a little cleft or rift in the mountain's flank—I found a thing which set the short hairs at the nape of my neck to bristling. There in the starlight were the marks of *El Lobo's* great splayed paws with the tiny footprints of my lost son, *moving side by side*. And that is the way those tracks disappeared into the darkness, down the mountain's wild and desolate slope."

I let the old man pause to think his own thoughts. I did not dare to break the slender thread which was leading him back through the years.

Presently, he sighed deeply and returned to those misty times.

"Long and weary was the trailing through that night," he said. "My men were several times at the edge of exhaustion, at the rebel's point of turning back. But, as I, they loved the boy. We staggered on, our horses now behind us, led by their bridles, the way too steep and treacherous for them to bear us.

"Dawn found us at our trail's end. And, yes, I see that you have guessed it: the trail brought up sharply at the very door of my own great hacienda. From that place, the giant tracks of the wolf faded back into the fastness of *El Trueno*.

"Frantically, I rushed into my house, only to be met and silenced by my servants and my women, who informed me that the boy had been snugly in his bed and sleeping these three hours!"

The old man frowned, moving his head uncertainly.

"The boy had simply come out of the blackest part of the dawn, saying he was tired and wanting to go to his bed. He seemed in no way disturbed by his harrowing experience.

"The following day, however, we noted an odd reluctance on his part to discuss, in any way, the adventure. That he had been with the wolf we could determine. He made several references to the 'big gray dog.' And we found upon his garments a great quantity of the black-tipped, silver guard hairs of the timber wolf. Indeed, it was as though the great brute and my son had lain down together to rest upon the trail at some point during their remarkable journey.

"Some time later the boy's behavior became more marked in its strangeness. We called in the priest, but he could gain no more from my son than could we, his parents and protectors. I have never since that day been the child of Mother Church that once I was. It seemed to me that here we were dealing with some very definite work of Lucifer, yet this bumbling *padre* could achieve no more than to thumb his beads and implore the Saints to send a sign by which he might know his way in the matter.

"Ah, what good is a God who will not better instruct his minions than that? Had I such a *mozo* or *peón* or *vaquero,* I would discharge him, or at least restrict his supply of *chiles* and *frijoles.* Well, I have wandered. Excuse me."

"It is nothing," I assured him. "All of these thoughts will pass through the mind in the remembering. I agree with you about priests. They eat too well. As you know, I am of the Faith, but I don't trust all these *padres.* I've known the sort you speak of. They ought to have been cart drivers, or charcoal burners, or again, *muleteros* or donkey women."

This pleased him fleetingly.

"Yes, they know more of boot soles than of human

souls. In any event, the boy became more and more peculiar. He was to be found from time to time in the extreme cold of the patio—winter was upon us now—clad only in his night clothes gazing away toward the mountain, his face lacking all mortal animation. When I questioned him somewhat sternly about these midnight forays, he only replied softly, 'He is calling me, Father; cannot you hear him up there upon the mountain?'

" 'Who is calling?' I demanded sharply, and he answered me, still looking far away:

" '*El lobo que llora, padre,* the wolf that cries.'

"It was hopeless—and very frightening. Each night the chill wail would come sobbing down from the heights of El Trueno. Sometimes the others of us could hear it, and sometimes we could not. But the boy heard it always.

"We attempted every device. Other priests were sent in from afar, even a bishop from Coahuila. Doctors we brought in from Socorro, Santa Fe, and even Las Cruces. What use? They charged us much money and left the boy no better. I have since felt about doctors as I do about *padres.* They should all have been carpenters, like the father of Jesus."

This was the last pause, now; one sensed it.

"Well, *señor,* you have been patient. It was on an eternally damned night, brief weeks later, that my son disappeared for the final time. But this time he did not leave alone. Leading from the door of my hacienda, clearly imprinted on the new-fallen snow, side by side with those small marks of my son's tiny feet, were the great pad marks of the wolf.

"We searched the mountain again the whole night

through, but you know the end, already, of this story. We did not find the boy; we did not find the wolf. Their trail faded into nothingness on the upper slopes of Thunder Mountain. The night was clear, the starlight blazing bright at this great height. Yet the tracks disappeared as if into the still black air.

"Nor did we ever find my son, *señor*. Stories there were, and continued to be: small frozen bodies found; tiny human skeletons revealed by the summer thaw high on the mountain; but always no real proof, always the body or the bones were gone when my riders and I came up to where they had been seen.

"After a certain time, my proud spirit died. My mind wandered, and my riches with it. Even my name was forgotten. It still is forgotten. These happy ones in this room do not remember me, only my story.

"It is as well. Do you know what night it was upon which the boy last left me, the night we found the wolf tracks leading him away from that door beyond the dancers, there? It was on the same night as this present one, *señor;* the same night and in this very hacienda, then mine, that it happened.

"Do you wonder, now, that I start up when *El Lobo* calls upon the mountain? Do you wonder that I hold my hand to my ear, listening to hear if it is my name he calls at last? Well, *señor*, the time of waiting is done. Tonight I heard my name. I am content, my friend. Already it grows over long since I have seen my little son. It will be a glad meeting on the far mountain. Remember that. Let there be no sadness, now, when the wolf has called again."

I started to say something to him, as his words

trailed off, but my own words never left my lips.

A log dislodged in the fireplace, sending up a shower of sparks. The noise of the revelers grew unaccountably quiet. I shook myself to ward off a sensation of creeping cold, or of a frosty draft of air. I even looked to see if some overheated dancers had opened the great oaken door of the hacienda. They had not.

Yet suddenly the merrymakers froze in their positions. A popping ember echoed in the stillness. From high above an eerily beautiful wolf howl sounded on Thunder Mountain. At the first notes of the call, the old man by my side glanced upward in the direction of El Trueno. But as the final strains sobbed from the heights, he was no longer looking toward the mountain. He was leaning back with a gentle smile of peace, and I realized the gallant soul had fled. There remained, however, one element of that departure which puzzled me. It was a thing I had to make sure of in my own mind, for the sake of my own peace.

I went quickly to the oaken door of the hacienda. When no one was watching, I opened it and stepped outside. A new snow was falling. It lay all about the ranch yard innocent of disturbance except for a singular distinct impression upon its starlit surface. From the hacienda's doorstep, stretching away into the winter darkness toward the waiting midnight snows of El Trueno, lay three sets of footprints: one set were those of a very old man, one those of a very young lad, and one those of a larger American timber wolf than I had ever seen.

Even as I stared at the ghostly footprints of the three companions, their trackmarks were beginning to fade beneath the increasing fall of the snow. When I returned to the big room of the hacienda and was told the old man had indeed passed on, I went again to the oaken door and looked out into the night.

The tracks were gone.

The snow beyond the ancient doorstep lay clean of any mark, and I never repeated this story, then or since.